A CHRISTMAS WITNESS

A CHRISTMAS WITNESS

CHARLES TODD

THE MYSTERIOUS PRESS
NEW YORK

A CHRISTMAS WITNESS

Mysterious Press
An Imprint of Penzler Publishers
58 Warren Street
New York, N.Y. 10007

Copyright © 2025 by Charles Todd

First Mysterious Press edition

Interior design by Charles Perry

All rights reserved. No part of this book may be reproduced in whole or in part without written permission from the publisher, except by reviewers who may quote brief excerpts in connection with a review in a newspaper, magazine, or electronic publication; nor may any part of this book be reproduced, stored in a retrieval system, or transmitted in any form or by any means electronic, mechanical, photocopying, recording, or other, without written permission from the publisher.

Library of Congress Control number: TK

ISBN: 978-1-61316-689-5

Ebook ISBN: 978-1-61316-690-1

10 9 8 7 6 5 4 3 2 1

Printed in the United States of America
Distributed by W. W. Norton & Company

Chapter One

LONDON, DECEMBER 1921: Rutledge had walked from his usual restaurant to his flat after dinner. The town was in the throes of Christmas preparations. Shop windows were brightly decorated with goods and gift suggestions, and streets in Town were crowded with people. And yet he could feel, this December, the sense of loss that permeated his being. So much of life in Britain had changed. There were the wounded on the street corners, begging. And more women in the shops than men of military age. Older women still wore the black of mourning for sons, brothers and husbands. Among them were young girls who were laughing and careless of passersby, enjoying an outing and the glances of anyone who would notice them.

Rutledge remembered Christmas of his childhood, not as gaudily celebrated as it was now. His father brought in an evergreen tree from a friend's farm and his mother decorated the tree with candles and bows. There was one present under the tree for him and one for his sister. The stockings were filled with oranges and nuts. His sister Frances loved the oranges most of all. Rutledge enjoyed Offering Day, which many people called Boxing Day. His parents did not have many servants of their own and would visit his father's clerks from his law practice. Carolers or wassailers would come to the house door making merry and his mother would give them the traditional figgy pudding.

Rutledge stopped his train of thought as he entered his flat when, no sooner than he had closed the door, a knock came. Assuming it was a neighbor or someone having a medical emergency Rutledge turned and opened the door. Practically filling the frame was a uniformed Metropolitan Policeman.

"A message for you, sir, from Chief Superintendent Markum."

Rutledge took the note from him and read the simple message.

Rutledge, something has come up and I require your presence in my office directly. Markum.

He politely thanked the officer, who was not to blame for whatever mess brought him out this evening.

Rutledge gathered his executive briefcase, the one that Melinda Crawford had given him when he was promoted to Chief Inspector, and hurried back down the stairs to his motorcar. As he set the ignition and cranked the engine to start, Rutledge wondered what Markum wanted at this hour. As far as he knew everything was well in hand when he left his tiny office earlier that day. There were promises of a larger office soon with his promotion, but that remained to be seen.

There were all sorts of motorcars and carriages out on the street and the cabbies were doing a brisk business. Eventually, Rutledge arrived at the offices of Scotland Yard. The New Scotland Yard since 1890, but it was still the Yard to those who worked there. Switching off his engine, Rutledge got down from his motorcar and headed toward the street entrance. This time of the year the Metropolitan Police was open all night. Greeting officers as he made his way up the stairs, Rutledge could see the light on in Markum's office.

"Good evening, Chief Superintendent. I came as quickly as I could. The holiday traffic is substantial this evening."

Without raising his eyes, Markum motioned Rutledge toward a chair in front of his desk. Markum was always busy with papers and Rutledge was accustomed to his lack of manners. At long last, Markum looked up from the pile in front of him and spoke.

"Yet, as you can see, the work of the Yard continues. I have a situation that requires your tact and patience."

Rutledge could feel himself sinking lower in his chair.

"We have received a complaint from the High Constable of Kent regarding Lord Braxton. Colonel Braxton. His name may ring a bell with you?"

"No, sir, I have no recollection of his name. There were so many in the Army in France."

"He is a close personal friend of Field Marshal Sir Douglas Haig. They attended Sandhurst together and served much of their careers together. Sir Haig had him on his personal staff during the Great War."

"I understand, sir. Little wonder we never crossed paths."

"Well, he had an accident he claims was caused deliberately and has a severe concussion. He is certain that someone is determined not to let him live to Christmas Day."

"What brought in the Yard?" Rutledge knew the answer, but he was trying to move this along to the matter that applied to him.

"Obviously, it is a sensitive matter that requires the utmost discretion. And in recognition of Lord Braxton's service to our country we are happy to oblige."

It was clear to Rutledge. It would be his obligation to happily represent the Yard.

Markum continued, "Lord Braxton is particular regarding who we send on this case. Your military service and position as a Chief Inspector were to Lord Braxton's liking."

Whenever Rutledge heard the record of his military service brought up, he became immediately tense and suspicious. While he had served successfully, resulting in his promotion to Captain, it was his injuries, especially the shell shock, that worried him. Maybe he could delay the trip.

"I am honored he found me satisfactory, although I may not be the person coming during the holidays. He will have family with him, and the person should be someone he knows."

"Oh no, my boy! You are the perfect fit for this job. You are not married and have no children to be with for Christmas. I understand this is an inconvenient time for us all, but I need you to get to Hartsham, Kent, as soon as possible. The Chief Constable said that while sometimes delirious due to his injury, he retains his military bearing."

Rising from his chair, Rutledge said, "In that case, I will return to my flat and put some things in a case for the trip."

Markum handed Rutledge a file. "This contains all the particulars that have come to me. Check in with the local constabulary and the Doctor on your way to the house."

"I assumed Sergeant Gibson would have all the information," Rutledge replied, taking the file from Markum.

"Not in this case. It's too sensitive. Let's not involve people who are not critical to the case. We have his Lordship's reputation to consider here."

Rutledge raised his eyebrow briefly but Markum did not elaborate.

"Report to me alone on this. And remember who you are going to see. I expect the reputation of the Yard to remain intact as well."

As soon as the door to Markum's office was closed, Rutledge looked back to see that he had sat back down and was working on his papers again.

Chapter Two

On his way back to his flat, Rutledge realized he had to make a telephone call if he was to be gone for Christmas. A part of him understood that being a single man with little family he was the easiest to call upon for a case at this time of year. It was also becoming obvious that being the newest Chief Inspector made him the one to get cases other more established Chiefs would not want.

After parking his motorcar, Rutledge stopped at the new cement telephone kiosk to place a call to his sister Frances. Her husband Peter answered the telephone with a hesitant voice.

"Hello, Peter. Rutledge here. Sounds like you are not accustomed to a telephone in the house."

"Confounded thing. How are you? We are looking forward to seeing you for Christmas."

"I am well, thank you, Peter. Sadly, I am calling with my apologies. I have been assigned a case in Kent and will be unable to attend Christmas with you and Frances."

There were some jostling noises from Peter's end of the line and Rutledge heard Frances's voice.

"Ian, whatever do you mean about missing Christmas with us!"

"Frances, I am very sorry, but I just got summoned to the office and was assigned a case in Kent."

"That's not far, is it? Surely you can still come for a visit even if it is brief. We miss you, Ian."

"I will see if I can get away, but you should know I may be busy with this case."

"I hope you get everything taken care of before Christmas. It will not be the same without you!"

"I will do my very best, I promise, Frances."

"All right then, be careful, and come see me soon!"

"Good night to you and Peter."

Rutledge disconnected the line and returned the earpiece to its cradle. He missed Frances, but she and Peter lived in his parents' house, which still brought difficult memories. Frances had yet to make the house her home and put her taste into the decor. Her life was now with her family with Peter. Soon, he expected news of a baby.

Rutledge went up to his flat and began packing his valise and placing his papers in his case. He knew his promotion to Chief Inspector was a gift due to the influence of Melinda Crawford, a friend of his family who had led a fascinating life in Africa and India with her late husband who was career Army. Over the years they had become quite close, but there were some effects from the war that he did not share with her.

Carrying his luggage down to his motorcar, he set it in the boot. With the engine cranked, Rutledge climbed up into his seat and pulled his coat out of the way before closing the door. The trip would not be very long, but the icy winter wind would make for a cold drive. As he left the city, Hamish spoke from his seat behind Rutledge.

"Ye ken this be a wild goose chase."

Rutledge was used to the voice in his head. It had been there since the summer of 1916, at the height of the battle of the Somme. It had been the bloodiest of battles, and men died before his eyes, day and night, until the trenches reeked of rotting flesh and black mud and death. He wasn't the only one on the verge of breaking as the Germans had pressed harder and harder, hoping to end the stalemate of 1915.

And then orders had come down to take out a German machine gun nest that was perfectly situated to halt the next British attack. But it was too well protected, and wave after wave of men had tried and failed to take it. Their wounded and their dead seemed to be piled high around them, and Corporal Hamish MacLeod had finally refused to lead another attack against the machine gun position. He pointed out what Rutledge had known from the start, that it was hopeless and a waste of good men. But the next attack was coming, and Rutledge was all too aware that the slaughter would be unimaginable if the first waves were caught in the open with that gun on their flank.

He had reasoned with Hamish, he had threatened, and it did no good. Hamish was as sick of the killing as Rutledge was and weary of dragging their dying wounded back to the trench. He had looked at the men who were left and said, "It is murder, pure and simple. I will na' do it anymore. I canna' do it anymore. No man in his right mind can justify it."

And with the next assault only hours away, coming with the dawn, Rutledge had had no choice but to make an example of his corporal before the rest of his men lost heart and refused to follow orders as well. Military necessity. The words still haunted him. The salient was buried a few minutes later, as the shelling began, softening up the German trenches before the advance. One shell fell short—and Rutledge, the firing squad, and his dead corporal had been buried in the explosion. Rutledge had been the lone survivor, and he only lived long enough to be dug out because his face had been pressed against the chest of the man he'd just executed. A tiny pocket of air . . .

Shell shock, it was called. Breaking under fire. But Rutledge couldn't accept that he'd been the sole survivor—or that the shell had come too late to stop the execution. Sacrificing one to save the many. And when the war was over, Hamish came home with Rutledge in the only way possible. Not as a ghost, not as a living man, but as a voice that haunted Rutledge night and day. A reminder of that night. Survivor's guilt, Doctor Fleming had called it. Seeing in Hamish MacLeod all the many dead he'd sent into battle, while he himself, always at their forefront, had hardly a scratch on him. A charmed life, his men had called it, only half joking . . .

"You and I know that, but someone must go," Rutledge said.

"Ye just wan' an excuse to miss Christmas. I'm onto ye," Hamish replied.

As they entered the countryside away from the city, Rutledge thought about what Hamish had said. Was he avoiding Christmas? Suddenly, Rutledge felt alone.

Having studied the maps, Rutledge made the turn east from the main road toward Maidstone. As he drove, the orchards were on either side of the road. Bare and lifeless, with limbs dotted with snow, they looked like hands reaching for the sun hoping for some warmth in the eerie dark. As he approached Maidstone, he began looking for signs to Hollingbourne toward the southeast. Hartsham and the Lord's estate was before one reached Hollingbourne but in the same direction.

Braking hard, Rutledge almost missed the sign for Hartsham in the darkness. Turning off onto the small road, it was not more than a few miles before he reached his destination. Hartsham was a typical small village in Kent with the High Street running through the center of town. Now it was too dark and late to see much of it. Everyone but Rutledge was tucked inside staying warm. Rutledge was glad for his heavy coat and scarf, but still the cold was getting to his bones, and he too needed to get inside and get warm. Turning left off the High onto West Street, Rutledge found an inn and pub named Percival's Rest.

Rutledge pulled into the parking area behind the building and cut off the ignition. Suddenly, the silence was deafening. If not for an occasional muffled sound of glasses and laughter, he would wonder if the place was open. In the dark it was hard to see the door, which seemed black, but he opened it and found a quiet neighborhood pub. Off to one side was a fireplace which Rutledge approached gratefully. It was good to feel the warmth of the fire when he removed his driving gauntlets and opened his coat.

"Your'n come in to warm yourself or did your'n want to order something?"

Rutledge turned to see a woman standing with her hands on her hips, but there was a glint in her eye that belied her tone.

"Yes, ma'am, a whisky, if you please."

"I'll bring it right over to ye in a jiffy."

Rutledge thanked her and watched her walk over to the barkeep. It was apparent he was the man to see for a room.

He handed her a glass and she put it on a small tray and returned in Rutledge's direction.

"Nary the finest ye ever had, but it will do on a cold night."

"Thank you, Miss . . . ?"

"Annie. And you, the London man, what is yer name?"

"Ian, I was wondering who to ask about a room for a few nights."

"Speak to Harold, he's the one minding th' bar tonight."

Taking a sip of his whisky, Rutledge replied, "The whisky is fine, Annie, and I will speak to Harold then," placing a coin on Annie's tray.

"I'll bring your change, Mr. Ian."

"No worry. Have one on me."

"Maybe later, thanks." And Annie was off to other customers.

Rutledge savored his whisky, while the fireplace did its work. He could tell from the men's clothing as he glanced around the room that this was an agricultural and industry town. They had been curious about the stranger who came in but were happily back to their conversations and a few laughs. After a few more minutes of warmth by the fire, Rutledge walked over to the bar.

He stood holding his glass in his hand, leaning on the bar as he waited for Harold to finish taking care of other customers. Finally, it was his turn.

"Another whisky, sir?"

"Yes, thank you. Annie said you were the man to see about rooms."

"Harold, at yer service. I'll pour you a whisky and we can talk."

Rutledge nodded and Harold reached for the whisky bottle and poured a healthier portion.

"How many nights were ye needin'?"

"I am not sure how long my business here will last. A few nights at least."

"We can take care of that. Ye got any bags to bring up to the room?"

"Only a valise and that is no trouble at all. I will bring it in."

"Well, have a sit down and I'll get the keys and all in a bit."

"Take your time, I'll take a stool here at the bar. Is there a place to hang my coat?"

Harold nodded his head toward a series of pegs near the door. "Ye can hang it right yonder."

"Thank you, Harold."

Rutledge stood up and took his coat off and put the scarf and driving gauntlets in the pockets. He went to the door and hung it on an available peg. Seated back at his stool, Rutledge took another sip of his whisky.

"They'll nary like ye when they ken who ye are," Hamish said.

Rutledge almost answered him out loud. Checking himself, he knew Hamish was right. Instead, he observed Harold. He was a tall, strong-looking man with his shirt sleeves rolled high above his elbows and a vest of sorts over his shirt. His ruddy complexion and brown hair made him look like someone to be reckoned with, especially in his establishment. Annie, on the other hand, was short in stature, with her piercing blue eyes and reddish hair. It was not her size that mattered as much as her take-no-prisoners attitude that made her the more formidable of the two of them.

Harold came over to Rutledge, "A room you'll be wanting then?"

"Yes, for a few days."

"All right then. Sign the register here." Harold laid a leather-bound registration book on the bar and opened it to the latest page.

Rutledge took out his pen from his waistcoat and looked at the information required. He remembered Markum saying, "Let's not involve people who are not critical to this case. We have his Lordship's reputation to consider here." So he completed the registration listing his flat address and occupation as simply, "Business."

"Here you go, Harold," Rutledge said pushing the register in his direction, replacing the cap on his pen before returning it to his waistcoat.

Harold glanced at the register and closed it before returning it to its place under the bar. He handed a key to Rutledge. "Top of the stairs on the left," he said nodding in the direction of the stairs.

"Thank you, I'll just finish my whisky and then bring my cases inside."

Rutledge savored his drink and the warmth before putting his coat back on and heading out into the cold to fetch his valise and briefcase. Once back inside, Rutledge headed up the small staircase to his room two doors down from the stairs. He stopped to try the door and found it was unlocked. Opening it, he found Annie putting a fresh pitcher of water below the washbasin.

"Ye startled me, begging your pardon, sir. I wanted you to have some fresh water."

"No trouble at all, Annie. I appreciate the effort at this hour."

"Well, ye have a good rest."

"Oh, Annie, what time is breakfast served?" Rutledge asked, trying to determine if they even served breakfast in Percival's Rest.

"Cook starts early, by six he should have everything ready for ye."

"Thank you, Annie, and a good night."

"You too," Annie said, closing the door behind her.

Rutledge opened his valise and turned to the wardrobe, opening the doors. He carefully laid his clothes on the shelves and hung his coat on one of the pegs opposite them. Next, he turned to the fireplace. Unlike the fireplace in the dining room downstairs, this was a coal grate with a bucket of coal set beside it on the hearth. A pair of tongs and a stoker leaned against its front. Annie had already set the fire, and it was putting out good heat. Rutledge removed his waistcoat, placing it on the only chair, and then sat on the bed with his briefcase. Taking out the files from Markum, Rutledge began to review the contents.

Lord Edward Braxton was born in 1860 and joined the Army in 1884, the same year as Sir Douglas Haig. They graduated in 1885 and were both assigned to the prestigious 7th Queen's Own Hussars. Braxton was commissioned as a lieutenant into this elite cavalry regiment, as was Haig. From there their paths crossed several times including in the Boer War from 1899 to 1902. In 1908 Haig called upon Braxton to work with his staff establishing the British Expeditionary Force in preparation for a European War. With the outbreak of war in 1914, Lord Braxton continued to serve on Haig's staff. When Haig became Commander in Chief of the British Expandatory Force in France at the rank of General, Lord Braxton remained on at the rank of Colonel. In 1919 Haig was promoted to Field Marshal by King George the Fifth and Lord Braxton served as a member of his staff at the Peace Talks.

Rutledge leaned back and rubbed his eyes.

"Yon Laird war on Butcher Haig's coattails!" Hamish remarked.

"No doubt about that," Rutledge replied.

Rutledge scanned over the rest of his file. Braxton inherited the Lordship from his father and the land associated with the estate. It sat in an area that was nestled on the edge of a forest with the tenant farms close to Hartsham. In the morning, he would see the ancestral home in the light of day. Gathering the papers and placing them in the folder from Markum, Rutledge placed the file back in his briefcase. He was glad he had replaced the wicker woven basket boot on his car with a metal lined boot that was bolted to the frame; it was important to him that his items in his boot were secure. Standing up and stretching, Rutledge prepared for bed.

A CHRISTMAS WITNESS

❄

Rutledge spent the night waking up from a recurring nightmare. During the war he had heard his Regimental Colonel lay out the plans for another round of going over the top. Rutledge knew better than to argue with the commanders. They were simply passing down the orders from above. In tonight's dreams he kept losing his temper and engaging in arguments with his superiors. Rutledge would feel his anger build to the point of physical confrontation before he woke up in a fit of rage. Each time he would go back to sleep the same series of events would repeat themselves. Finally, at dawn, Rutledge got up and put some coal on the grate to burn the chill off the room. He prepared his clothes and filled the washstand with freezing cold water, the ice now melted. After his washup, Rutledge got dressed with Hamish hammering away at him.

"Ye ken ye're upset meeting the friend and member o' Butcher Haig's staff."

"The war is over and that is in the past. It has nothing to do with the case at hand."

"True, but ye canna' hide yer feelings."

Dressed, with case in tow, Rutledge headed down to breakfast.

Entering the dining room, he saw a young woman waiting on the few early risers. Once Rutledge settled into his chair, she came over.

"What can I serve ye this morning?"

Rutledge looked up at her and saw she was in her early twenties with the same reddish hair and piercing blue eyes that Annie had. He wondered if she was a daughter or younger sister.

"A pot of tea and some porridge with some toast, please."

"I'll have it right out, with the tea first."

"That will do nicely," Rutledge replied.

Reaching down to his case, Rutledge took out the file Markum had given him the night before. Lord Braxton was married to Louisa in 1897. Louisa was from another military family, and they met while he was attending Sandhurst and then again when he was attending the Staff College, Camberley, in 1896. They had corresponded ever since they met in 1874.

Rutledge deftly closed the file as the young woman brought out the tea.

"Would ye like some milk or sugar with yer tea?" she asked.

"No, thank you, I like it as it is."

"Suit yourself. Yer porridge will be along in a minute," she said as she turned to head back to the kitchen.

Looking at his watch, Rutledge saw he just had time to eat before visiting the Constable and the Doctor. Then he could arrive at Cottams House to see Lord Braxton at a decent hour.

"Ye're delaying what ye dread," Hamish chided.

"I certainly am not." Rutledge looked around to see if he had responded out loud.

After finishing his breakfast, Rutledge put on his coat and headed toward the High. Here too the shop windows were all decorated for the holidays with children gazing through the glass and people going from place to place. Even Hartsham had holiday shoppers and various business people on the street. Rutledge was looking for a constable among the people on the High. Soon enough he saw the familiar custodian's hat. Rutledge approached the man and spoke to catch his attention.

"Good morning, Constable."

The man turned and replied, "Borough Police, and a good morning to you."

Rutledge produced his identification and said, "I was not aware Hartsham was a borough."

Glancing at Rutledge's identification, the officer replied, "Maidstone Borough Police, we cover this area. The name is Officer James Wilson, at your service, Chief Inspector."

"I was called in to investigate Lord Braxton's injury. Do you know which officer was contacted when it happened?"

"That would be me, Chief Inspector," Officer Wilson said with a bit of a grin.

"Can you tell me what happened?"

"Well, sir, it was over when I arrived, and Lord Braxton was already taken back inside the manor. Apparently, he was out walking after breakfast when a horseman ran him down. The metal horseshoe clipped his head and he has a pretty serious injury."

"Let's step into this teahouse if you have time. I need a full report," Rutledge said, gesturing toward a small tea shop there on the High.

"I always have time for a cuppa. Lead the way, sir," Officer Wilson replied.

Chapter Three

They stepped off the High and into the local tea shop. Taking a seat by the front window, Rutledge ordered a pot of tea from a polite lady who disappeared to fetch it. Officer Wilson clearly knew her and they exchanged greetings, though he declined to introduce Rutledge, for which Rutledge was grateful.

"As I was saying, sir, there was naught to tell really. Lord Braxton was inside and the Doctor was with him."

"Who was the Doctor who tended to him?" Rutledge asked, because Markum had instructed him to meet with the Constable and the Doctor before meeting Lord Braxton.

"Old Doc Wright, he has a home on West Street with a practice in the front," Wilson replied. "Just down from the post office, number Sixty-Two West Street. His practice is two doors down with a blue door."

"I think I know the post office; I am staying at Percival's Rest on West Street."

"Yes, the post office is across the street from there."

"I hope to speak to him on my way to Cottams House."

"Ol' Doc Wright is a good man. You will find him at home at this hour seeing patients. Lord Braxton is another matter."

"How so?" Rutledge asked raising an eyebrow.

"He's a retired Army man. Impatient and demanding he is. His wife Lady Braxton is a very gracious lady."

"I know the type from France."

"In the war then, sir?"

"I was in the trenches, but I met some of the senior officers. Not Lord Braxton, but the type."

"He goes by Colonel and was in the Second Boer War before returning to London where he worked with Haig starting up the BEF."

Rutledge knew the British Expeditionary Force was begun in 1906 and Haig was responsible for setting it up. Things were becoming unsettled in Europe even then.

"Did you go out to where Lord Braxton was injured?"

"I did, it was a mix of mud and snow. There were a lot of tracks after they came for Lord Braxton; mostly though, they were lost in the mud."

"What about the direction the rider came and left?"

"That was odd, I could na find anything indicating where the rider came from or went to. Mind you, the sun was melting the snow by the time I got there. The household was more concerned with getting Lord Braxton moved and seen to."

"What alerted the household?" Rutledge inquired.

"One o' the grounds keeps was out and about checking on things. He heard the Lord cry out and came a runnin'."

"What was the grounds keep's name?"

"Lemme see," The officer reached inside his uniform coat and drew out a standard officer's log. "Yes, Arthur Steves is the one. Been there nigh on twenty years. Too old for the war he was. He oversees the grounds as sort of a game warden."

Rutledge finished up his cup of tea and rose from his chair, putting some coins on the table. "Thank you for your help, Officer Wilson. As I said, I am staying at Percival's Rest and you can leave word there if you need anything."

The officer stood and extended his large hand to Rutledge. "I am out of East Maidstone and you can reach me there. I usually make several patrols in the area. You can leave word at this tea shop if you need me."

Rutledge nodded and headed back out on the High.

"He likes the tea shop and the lass workin' thar," Hamish said.

Rutledge muttered a reply and made his way back to Percival's Rest and his motorcar. Setting his case in the front seat, Rutledge set the ignition and went around to crank the motor. Climbing in behind the steering, Rutledge headed out onto West Street. Turning left, the post office and shop was on his right and shortly the blue door of Doctor Wright came into view. Like most of the houses it was a brick terraced house with a bay front window and a sash window on the opposite side of the door. There was a low wrought iron fence with brick corners in front of the house with a small cement patio. It was a two-story house with an overhang above the door, also in brick, and a lamp by the front door.

Parking on the curb, Rutledge switched the ignition off and got down. The brick had been warmed by the morning sun. Rutledge knocked at the door and it was soon opened by a woman in a nursing uniform.

"Do come in, sir. Can I take your coat?"

"Yes, thank you." Taking off his coat and handing it to the nurse, Rutledge said, "I was wanting a word with Doctor Wright, if he is available."

"He is with a patient but will be available shortly. Who shall I say is calling?"

"Chief Inspector Rutledge from Scotland Yard," Rutledge replied, showing her his identification.

"Yes, sir, right away. Please have a seat and I will let the Doctor know you are here."

As the nurse went toward the back rooms, Rutledge left the foyer and entered the sitting room to wait. It was nicely decorated with both plush and wooden chairs. There was a serviceable rug on the floor with a simple pattern and a round table in the center of the room. The wall was papered in ivory paper with light green lines and ivy; it was more of a waiting room than a sitting room, and what he had seen so far of the house was sterile. The few lamps on side tables were redundant, with the sun beginning to come through the bay window.

It was not very long before a woman came out from the back rooms and thanked the nurse before making her way to the door and putting on her coat. The nurse came into the room where Rutledge was waiting and informed him the Doctor was available, and to follow her. Returning to the foyer the nurse lead Rutledge past the staircase and stopped to knock at a door.

"Come," said a deep voice from within, and the nurse opened the door to a room set up as an office. The large rolltop desk was against the wall and an older man turned his swivel chair to greet him. The room was darker than the sunlit front of the house. There was a lamp on the desk and another on an older Victorian style side table. On the wall above the desk were diplomas in need of dusting indicating Doctor Wright's graduation from medical school.

"Chief Inspector, how may I be of help to you today?" the Doctor said in greeting.

"I understand that Lord Braxton is a patient of yours and you were called to the house after yesterday's incident. The Yard sent me to look into this matter."

"The Yard, you say. Well, I knew that Lord Braxton was a Colonel during the war. Chief Inspector, did you say?"

"Yes, the Yard was contacted by the Chief Constable," Rutledge explained. "I was instructed by my superior to come straight away. What can you tell me about the incident at Lord Braxton's home?"

The Doctor stretched his long arms and legs. He was an older man, but spry in his manner. "I was called out to Cottams House midmorning. By the time I got there they had already moved him into the house and up to his bedchamber. I removed the bandages they used to staunch his bleeding head wound. I cleaned it up. There was a lot of mud in the wound and about his face. A cut above his right eyebrow was deep enough to partially expose the skull. There is not much between the skin and bone in that area. I sewed it closed with about a dozen stiches and bandaged it properly. In fact, before your arrival delayed me, I was getting ready to leave for Cottams House to check on Lord Braxton's recovery."

"I was heading there after seeing you first. My motorcar is at the curb. You are welcome to ride with me."

"While I appreciate your kind offer, it will be best if I let you follow me. I have other patients to check on after Lord Braxton."

"Before we go to the house, I would appreciate your insight into his mental faculties. Were they impaired from the wound?"

"Ah, that is a bit of a sticky wicket there. Lord Braxton is definitely a military man and not one to complain. However, he received a concussion, which has resulted in a bit of confusion. I learned more about the incident from the groundskeeper than Lord Braxton. The only thing Lord Braxton said was someone tried to kill him with a horse. He was quite insistent that someone was out to kill him. He was a bit delirious, and I gave him a sedative in hopes he would sleep. The brain is something that still mystifies us. Experience tells me that sleep is the best medicine for the brain to heal itself."

"What did the wound tell you? Is the cause of his wound supported by any medical certainty?"

"Did his description match the injury? Is that what you are asking?"

"Precisely, Doctor. You said he was delirious and unable to communicate due to his injuries."

"That is hard to determine. As I said there was mud in the wound and around his face. Still, I am a bit concerned with your question. Lord Braxton is a highly respected member of this community. Far be it for me to question his veracity!"

"I would never question his word, Doctor. You said that he was delirious and that led to my question. I am simply attempting to understand the facts."

"I understand and respect your processes. His wound could have been caused by a horseshoe striking his head with a glancing blow. Had the horseshoe struck him directly, I doubt you would be asking Lord Braxton anything at all."

"Thank you, Doctor. I meant no disrespect with my questions; I hope you understand that I had to ask."

"Not a worry, Chief Inspector. Let's go to the house and you can see Lord Braxton for yourself. I have to change his bandages and you will see the wound," the Doctor said, rising from his chair.

Rutledge was surprised how tall the Doctor was when he stood. His lanky frame was obvious even in his chair, but he was a very tall man. The two went to the foyer where the nurse was at the ready with their coats.

"I am parked around the back, so I will come around on the street. Then you can follow me," the Doctor informed Rutledge.

Rutledge nodded and then headed to the street. By the time the Doctor's motorcar came around the corner Rutledge was already in his seat with the engine running. The Doctor was driving an Austin 7hp from about 1910. It was small, but it obviously got him where he needed.

Chapter Four

The Doctor headed toward the High. Then, crossing the High, he headed on to East Street. The village and the terraced houses and businesses gave way to individual stone houses and a few warehouses on the left. Before long, the buildings were behind them with a tree bank on the left and open fields on the right side of the road. The road began to wind its way through the hedgerows, with a few houses here and there. At times, the trees formed a tunnel with their leafless branches forming a cover over the road.

The cars slowed and turned right onto a small country road that wound its way across the countryside eventually coming to a wrought iron double gate supported by rock gate posts and a wall that extended along the road in front of what Rutledge imagined would be a beautifully manicured lawn—if it weren't covered in snow—before returning to the hedgerows. Rutledge followed the Doctor through the gate and as they crested a slight rise, the house itself could be seen: an Elizabethan exposed-timber house with high arched roofs. The windows were typical of that style, wide and extending from the ceiling to the floor of each story. The drive rolled gently down, forming a circle in front of the house with a fountain in the center that was covered for the winter. Doctor Wright pulled his motorcar to a stop in front of the house and turned off the ignition. He was unfolding his tall frame out of his Austin as Rutledge pulled up behind him. Together they approached the front entrance with its carved dark wood that matched the timbers of the house.

Doctor Wright's drawing on a chain resulted in the clang of a bell inside. The door opened and a uniformed butler swung it wide.

"Doctor Wright, his Lordship is expecting you," the butler said, stepping back with the door in his hand motioning the Doctor inside.

"Good morning, Davies. Allow me to introduce Chief Inspector Rutledge from Scotland Yard."

"Good morning, sir. Please allow me to take your coats."

A young woman appeared at the bottom of the narrow set of stairs coming down to the foyer.

"Miss Violet will take you up to his Lordship's bedchambers," Davies explained.

"Thank you," Rutledge said and turned to follow the Doctor and Violet up the stairs.

At the top of the stairs, Violet turned right and led them down the hallway.

The house was as Elizabethan in the interior as it was outside. The tall ceilings and exposed rafters of the entry gave way upstairs to low ceilings and dark wood walls. The dark burgundy carpet made the sense of darkness complete. The ceiling was a flat white with horizontal exposed timbers. Only the dim light from the wall sconces gave some light to the hall. At the end of the hallway Violet stopped at a door, knocked, and waited until the male voice inside said, "Come."

Opening the door wide, Voilet announced, "Doctor Wright and Chief Inspector Rutledge from Scotland Yard, your Lordship."

"About damn time. What kept you, Rutledge? We were expecting you last night," said the man propped up against pillows. The room was filled by a canopy bed with the sashes pulled back. The light from the open curtains brilliantly flooded the space.

Rutledge paused in surprised. The walls were covered in white wallpaper with burgundy crests surrounded by olive branches. The rest of the furniture was a light green and the red tile floor was covered with an oriental carpet in ivory. A small fire burned in the fireplace. It was an interesting mixture of the old and the new.

"Your Lordship, that is no way to welcome your guest," said Doctor Wright with a slight smile. Turning to Rutledge, he said, "He is not always this out of sorts."

"I am, sir. And I ask again, what kept you, young man?"

Rutledge replied, "It was late last night when I arrived in Hartsham. Considering your injuries, I thought it best to arrive at a decent hour this morning."

"In the future, when I call someone, I expect prompt attention," Lord Braxton said.

"Edward, my dear, you are being rude. Please remember this man is not some corporal," came a voice from the door.

Rutledge turned and there was a woman about the same age as his Lordship.

"Pardon me," she said entering the room. "I am Lady Braxton. I appreciate you coming all the way from London to help with this matter."

Taking her extended hand Rutledge wasn't certain if he should bow. Lady Braxton was a graceful woman with graying hair that was immaculately drawn up in a typical Edwardian style. Her blouse was silk with a high neck and an intaglio at her throat. Her skirt went down to the floor and was a classic gold and green. Her eyes showed both patience and intelligence. There was something else there that Rutledge could not place.

"It is a pleasure to meet you, your Ladyship," Rutledge said with a nod and no bow. Looking into her gaze, he noticed her soft brown eyes revealed a gentle nature.

Turning to Lord Braxton, Rutledge asked, "How are you feeling today, sir?"

"I am feeling better, but not a good as I should if I knew what progress you have made."

"I met with Officer James Wilson this morning. Unfortunately, the ground was trampled and the snow had muddied the crime scene. I was hoping you could fill me in while Doctor Wright sees to your bandages. Then, I will inspect the scene to see if anything was missed."

"That man is from East Maidstone, not from around here. His cursory evaluation has no bearing in this matter," Lord Braxton replied. "Hurry along, Doctor, I am no china doll," he admonished the Doctor.

"That is the last of the bandages, your Lordship. Now, turn toward the light so I can see what we have here."

Rutledge leaned forward to observe the wound. It was not ragged at all. Either the stiches were hiding any signs of another cause, or it was indeed a cut from a sharp object.

"See, young man, here is the wound. What do you deduce from that?" Lord Braxton asked.

"It looks like you had a very traumatic encounter. What can you tell me about the events that resulted in this happening?"

"I am getting tired of telling this every time you people come by asking the same questions."

"Frankly, your Lordship, I was hoping that with a good night's rest, the sequence of the events might be clearer than yesterday."

Doctor Wright straightened from bending over his bandages. "You still need some rest, your Lordship. I recommend bed rest, and I will come back tomorrow morning. How is the pain?"

"I have had enough fussing and worrying about pain. I want my mind clear so this young man will be satisfied. I have been through worse, as you well know!"

"I will leave some medicine with her Ladyship, and she can administer some to help you rest this evening," Doctor Wright said, looking up at Lady Braxton.

"I will see to it. And thank you, Doctor Wright," Lady Braxton responded.

Doctor Wright again spoke. "Well, your Lordship, I will leave you with the Chief Inspector here. Do not hesitate to telephone if you have any changes."

"Come with me, Doctor, and I will see you out," Lady Braxton said and turned to Rutledge. "I trust you will not over-tire the Colonel, Chief Inspector."

Doctor Wright nodded to Rutledge and they took their leave.

"Do you mind if I sit here at your side, your Lordship?" Rutledge asked.

"Only if you call me Colonel, and let this Lordship go," the Colonel replied.

Rutledge pulled a wooden chair up to the side of the bed with the window on the opposite side of the Colonel and took out his notebook from his topcoat. "Please pardon the notes I take. They are for the facts surrounding yesterday's incident."

The Colonel practically growled his displeasure but gave no argument.

Hamish had been right, there was a feeling of resentment in Rutledge toward this man. Here he was, sitting close to one of those who sent so many young men to die.

"Or came back like you," Hamish was ringing in his mind.

Rutledge reminded himself why he became a policeman. He was investigating murders and bringing killers to justice. His strong belief in right and wrong guided his work. He had risen to Chief Inspector in spite of his own troubles and superiors who resented him. Now was the time to help this man who thought he was being targeted by a killer. Whoever this rider was who charged at the Colonel was certainly not like Hamish. Hamish warned Rutledge when there was danger, he was a part of him that he'd brought back from the war. While Hamish delighted in goading Rutledge with his comments and sometimes harsh words, Hamish was still the man that Rutledge had executed and would be with him in any room, now and always. Rutledge knew that Hamish would never hurt him. No, the person who charged the Colonel with his horse was nothing like Hamish. From the Colonel's description, his attacker was very much alive.

"Let's start at the beginning, in your words. I have second- and thirdhand accounts, but you are the one who was there and best able to describe what occurred," Rutledge began.

"Understand young man, I have recited this story and gone over it in my mind so many times. Louisa, Lady Braxton, has been anxious and I have tried to spare her," the Colonel said.

"I do understand. It is rare for me to have the opportunity to speak with you. Many of my cases involve victims who cannot speak for themselves. I also appreciate why you would wish to keep Lady Braxton from being worried with the gruesome details. You are talking to me now. You can confide in me, trusting your thoughts and impressions will remain between us," Rutledge explained.

"Trust is earned, not given lightly. I just met you and baring my soul is not in my nature."

Rutledge did not respond. Sitting where he was, he waited for the Colonel to begin.

At last, the Colonel sighed and began his recollections. "After breakfast, it is my habit to walk the property and check in with my groundskeeper. Have you met Arthur Steves?"

"No, sir. I have been told that he found you first, alerted by your calling out. The Borough Policeman James Wilson had it in his report."

"I am surprised that man paid that much attention to the matter. Arthur has been with this estate for many years. He is getting older, but he is committed to his work and my family. I was walking away from the road along a line of trees when suddenly a horseman came out of the wood at a gallop. He intentionally ran me down. Could have killed me."

"What made you think he intentionally ran you down?"

"His horse came out of the woods, and he worked the reins, turning the horse directly toward me, giving it the spur. I cannot describe his face but those eyes were black with rage under his hunt-style helmet."

"You keep horses here at Cottams House?"

"Of course I do, but it was not one of my horses. I would have recognized it immediately."

"And you were on foot, correct?"

"Yes, damn you. Do you want this diatribe or not? You keep interrupting me!"

"My apologies, I won't interrupt you again. Please continue."

"His horse seemed to balk at the direction he was being steered in, just before it hit my head with the horseshoe. After that, I do not remember much. I might have lost consciousness or just been dazed. Oh, I do remember hearing the horse continue at a gallop off into the distance. It was a bit vague, but I am certain I remember it."

"You said you did not see the rider's face. Was there anything about him that seemed familiar?" Rutledge asked.

"He was dressed in a hunting habit, with white jodhpurs and woolen shirt with a high neck under his jacket. He had riding boots on with a riding crop in his hand. I did not recognize the horse or rider."

"You seem certain it was a man riding the horse."

"Do not you think I can tell the difference? Do not be ridiculous."

"This time of year, with heavy clothes and the hair hidden by a hunt-style helmet?"

"It was a man, I am certain."

"We always ask if someone wants you dead."

"Young man, there are plenty of people who would like me dead. Being in command, the men must hate you as much as the enemy. You were in the war, I know. Did you not think I would read your file before you arrived?"

Rutledge felt Hamish saying, "'Ware." Hamish, with his Scottish brogue, knew danger was afoot. Rutledge wondered how much of his record the Colonel knew.

"Of course you would, as I read about you. It comes with the job, sir," Rutledge replied, trying to seem matter-of-fact, while feeling the walls of the bedchamber closing in. His dislike of closed spaces came from his experience buried with Hamish by the shell. The size was not the concern as much as the feeling of being trapped. His file might place him in a difficult position if the Colonel had the right paperwork.

"Well then, we have that in common."

"Colonel, I meant something local or more specific. A person from here or some threats recently."

"It is odd that I did not recognize the horse. A chestnut horse with a black mane and tail. It carried itself in an unusual manner. I would have recognized that horse. Do you ride?"

"I have of course, but not for events or polo."

"Then you know how horses are different in their manner and the way they move. As I said, if I had seen that horse before, I would have remembered it!" the Colonel said. "As for threats, I am respected and have no real enemies in these parts. Of course, there are people who wish me ill. Widows and families, former soldiers, and that lot. Nothing specific."

Rutledge thought for a moment and then asked, "Any unusual correspondence in the past, say, month? Perhaps not a threat, more of a curious nature?"

The Colonel thought for a minute, and then said, "Not correspondence. I was in London for some meetings about the peace settlement and overheard someone saying something."

"I respect this is confidential, but please tell me what he said," Rutledge looked up from his notes.

"An aide de camp was boasting to his fellow officers that people such as Haig and those on his staff would be the

Jacob Marleys to the commanders of any new conflict. He was speaking out of place, passing judgment like that. Do you remember Dickens's story *A Christmas Carol*?"

"Naturally, it's well-known," Rutledge responded.

"So, you know that Marley was dead, and had died many years before. I took the aide de camp's comment to mean I would be dead. Who knows what he really meant. It is easy to challenge a commander's decisions after the fact. We had to make hard decisions without the hindsight our junior officers have. I am not about to apologize for the choices Haig and our staff made."

"Ye kenned what ye were gonna face when ye took this case," Hamish laughed harshly.

"I understand your feelings. We all faced our challenges during that ugly war. I am focused on this rider and what caused him to charge his horse at you."

"I am well aware of your responsibilities, young man. You asked me if I had any correspondence or anything unusual had happened," the Colonel angrily replied.

"Obviously, it came to mind. How long ago did this happen?"

"It was a few weeks ago, but it has stuck with me. I do not know why. Impertinence, of course. For some reason it had me thinking about Christmas when I was a boy and young man."

"Was Christmas a time of year that you and your family enjoyed?" Rutledge asked.

"It was not what it is these days. It was a simpler time. We had stockings hung on the fireplace with simple things such as nuts and oranges. A present from my parents and a traditional meal with goose and the trimmings. Sticky pudding naturally." A slight smile came over the Colonel.

Rutledge nodded in agreement, remembering his own earlier musings.

"And, what about this year's celebrations?"

"I have called it off. After this mad man tried to kill me, I have no appetite for frivolous holiday things. At this rate, I doubt I will be alive."

"Surely, sir, you are a fit man of good health. What would make you doubt you will not live for the next few days?" Rutledge said, as he forced himself to converse with one of the men who had planned his own troubles.

"I feel certain that man or those men are determined not to see me live. So I have informed the household there will be no Christmas this year. Louisa, er, Lady Braxton was not pleased, but after I am gone, she can do as she wishes."

"I am certain they care for you and will accept your decision. Would you like me to post some guards for the house?"

"If someone is coming for me, he will certainly outwit any guards. I do not want a false sense of security," the Colonel replied.

"As you wish. But if you are concerned for your safety at least let me and a few others from the Borough Police keep an eye on the property," Rutledge offered.

"I do not care if you take up lodgings here in the house. It will not be worth your energy when you need to resolve this matter," the Colonel replied angrily.

"You have had a full day, sir. Leave everything to me and I will come see you again tomorrow," Rutledge said, rising from his chair and replacing his notebook in his coat pocket.

"I am a bit tired, but I will expect a full report in the morning," the Colonel said, dismissing Rutledge with a wave.

"Thank you. I will make certain we stay outside the house, and I will keep my lodgings in the town. Will that be acceptable?"

"Whatever you wish," Lord Braxton said.

"I will see you tomorrow, sir."

Rutledge retraced his steps from earlier and returned to the foyer. The butler Davies met him with Rutledge's coat and helped him put it on.

"I need to see the groundskeeper. Steves, I believe."

"Yes, sir. You will see him out front near the gate. We are taking every precaution," Davies replied.

"Thank you, Davies, I will see you tomorrow if not before," Rutledge said, turning to the door.

"Oh, sir, Lady Braxton asked me to inform you that she had household business to attend to and is not able to see you off. She sends her apologies."

"Thank you, Davies. Please tell Lady Braxton that I am staying at Percival's Rest and to send word there if anything occurs or if either Lord or Lady Braxton require my attention."

"Yes, sir," Davies said, holding the door open for Rutledge.

Rutledge thought about starting the engine of his motorcar and driving to the gate and then changed his mind. The sun was out and it was not so cold as when he had followed the Doctor down the drive. Donning his gloves and adjusting his scarf, Rutledge stopped at his motorcar and took his Wellingtons out and put them on. Then he began to walk along the drive toward the gate.

Chapter Five

The nicely groomed lawn covered in its blanket of snow gave way to trees on either side. Rutledge could just glimpse some orchards and fields in the distance. Coming over the crest of the drive, the gate up at the road came into view. Rutledge could see the groundskeeper, Arthur Steves, bent over by the gate working on something, his shotgun leaning against the wrought iron fence. Rutledge spoke out as he approached the man.

"Hello, Steves is it?" Rutledge made certain he spoke loud enough for the groundskeeper to hear him, even as he was still a distance away. With the wounded Lord in the house and everyone on the alert, Rutledge did not wish to suddenly be looking down the barrels of a shotgun.

Steves gave something an additional touch and then stood to turn toward Rutledge.

"Yes, sir. You must be the man from London," Steves said in greeting.

Steves was about the same age as the Colonel. He had the look of a man who spent his time out and around the estate. His skin was still tanned from a combination of years in the sun and wind. He wore an eight-panel cap and a heavy Mackinaw coat that was open, revealing a lined duck cloth vest with a work shirt and tie. His corduroy pants and Wellingtons gave him a look of a gamekeeper more than a simple groundskeeper.

"I am indeed. Chief Inspector Rutledge from Scotland Yard," Rutledge said as he got close enough to extend his hand.

Steves shook his hand and asked, "What can I do fer ye, sir?"

Rutledge found it interesting that Chief Inspector was a mouthful for some when Inspector was not.

"I understand you were the first person to come to his Lordship's aid yesterday."

"Aye, I was out checking the grounds when I heard him holler out."

"Where exactly were you when you heard his Lordship?"

"I call him Colonel. He doesn't like to use his title," Steves said.

"Yes, he told me the same. So where were you when you heard the Colonel?"

"I was right over yonder," Steves said, pointing to the left side of the house.

"Could you walk me over there and then the path you took when you came to the Colonel's aid."

"Gimme a minute to finish this gate hinge. I figure they will be closing it at night now." Rutledge was surprised that the gate was not always in good repair, with all the visitors and the usual comings and goings at the estate. It made no sense for the gate needing any preparation due to the Colonel's injury that Steves would not have made the night before. Knowing how demanding the Colonel could be and the appearance of the immaculate grounds, why would the gate suddenly need repairs?

"Certainly, can I be of assistance?" Rutledge inquired.

"I am almost finished," Steves said, bending down again by the gate but not appearing to hurry.

Looking back at Rutledge, he added, "You're nary dressed for this work."

Rutledge smiled inwardly. If Steves had any idea what Rutledge had done dressed as he was, he would not have worried so much.

Steves finally straightened and looked down at his work with pleasure.

"All right then, let's be off to where this all happened."

Steves led the way across to the tree-lined edge of the lawn. Rutledge was glad he wore his Wellingtons. The snow had begun to melt and the ground the sun was shining upon was warming up and had begun to be mixed into mud. They followed the tree line until it opened and there was a meadow with a brook. Here the mud became treacherous and both men had to mind their step, though it was not far before Steves stopped.

Pointing to a spot on the ground, Steves said, "There is where I found the Colonel."

Rutledge could see the place where the Colonel had obviously laid. There were tracks in the snow where the Borough Policeman and several others had left their marks.

"So, it was here that you found the Colonel on the ground wounded?"

"Aye, right there," said Steves.

Not wanting to mix his tracks with the others, Rutledge carefully examined the area.

"I do not imagine there is any blood, but let me see what I can find."

"Thar warn't much except where his head laid," Steves said.

"Can you point to where his head was on the ground?" Rutledge said, not wanting any more confusing tracks in the area.

"Right thar," Steves said pointing to an area.

Rutledge stepped as close as he could. There was not much to see with the melting snow and mud. He had expected that. He remembered how the blood would soak into the ground from his time in the trenches. Bodies were all around him then, and yet the blood either all ran into the area away from the corpses or soaked into the ground. He remembered the wintertime when the blood was thick and stayed with the bodies. A close inspection of the place Steves said the Colonel's head laid, there was some matting on the ground, but no traces of any blood. Rutledge circled the area, again treading as lightly as he could making ever widening circles as he went. He was looking for horseshoe prints in the snow.

"Steves, was the Colonel conscious and able to speak when you found him?"

"He was dazed and mumbling a bit at first, and then he became quiet," Steves replied.

"I would imagine. That was quite a blow he took," Rutledge replied as he continued to widen his circles.

It was not long before his circles came to the tree line. Rutledge began focusing his attention on the trees. He paused from time to time looking at the tree bark, roots, and branches.

Surely, if a horse came bounding out of the trees there would be some broken branches at the very least,

Rutledge thought to himself. He looked back at the spot where the Colonel laid on the ground and looked at his notes. The Colonel said the rider steered his horse directly at him.

"Steves, do you see any broken branches or marks on these trees from a rider coming out of the trees?"

Steves came over to where Rutledge was standing and began looking along the tree line as well.

After a thorough examination, Steves said, "I don't see nary a mark, but ye see the branches have sap in 'em." Steves took a branch and bent it. The branch sprung back when he released it.

Rutledge turned back to the area where Steves had come upon the Colonel. Looking at the area again, he found what he was searching for but said nothing to Steves. In his notes Rutledge sketched a map of the area where the Colonel had laid and the area around it, including the tree line. It took time and a bit of patience, but it was not as hard as when he had to sketch the face of a dead man on a previous case. Rutledge finished drawing and made a few more notes and then turned to Steves.

"Thank you, Steves, you have been a great help. I understand you have been here many years?"

"Aye, nigh on twenty years or so. It's good work and I enjoy being outside, even when it's cold."

"Are there many orchards on the estate grounds?"

"Oh aye, we have several acres of orchards round behind the house. Ye can't see them from the house. Mainly apple orchards."

"Will there be any wassailing for the holidays around here, some house-visiting wassail?"

"Thar is some, especially from the village church," Steves replied.

"Interesting," Rutledge said and they began walking back to the drive and the front of the house. "Oh, is there much foxhunting here abouts?"

"Thar is the Boxing Day Meet about twenty miles from here, that will be in a few days."

"Really? I remembered that foxhunting was big to the west in Surrey," Rutledge replied, raising his eyebrows.

"They have been foxhunting in Kent since 1617," Steves replied matter-of-factly.

"I see. Anyone from the area involved?"

"My brother-in-law raises foxhounds."

"How about riders in the hunt?"

"They are mainly from the estates and manor houses in West Kent and East Surrey, about ten miles from here."

They arrived at the drive near where Rutledge had parked his motorcar.

"That's a nice motorcar ye have there, a '14, is it?"

"Yes, I have had it for a few years now, just before the war," Rutledge replied.

"A good traveling motorcar then," Steves remarked.

"It is that," Rutledge replied. "Thank you for your help and guidance today. I am sure I will be seeing you again over the next few days."

"And a good day to ye too," Steves said as he turned and walked away.

Rutledge leaned on the boot he had opened while he took off his Wellingtons and put his regular dress boots back on. They would need a good cleaning after all that snow and mud. Closing the boot, Rutledge went to the driver's side and turned on the ignition so he could crank the engine.

Rutledge headed toward the gate and Steves was there and waved. Returning the wave, Rutledge turned left and followed his way back toward Hartsham.

Chapter Six

"War it a horse or that stone, the Laird struck his head?" Hamish asked from the back seat behind Rutledge, his usual place.

Rutledge had sworn that if he ever saw Hamish, he would end his life at last. Rutledge never tried to see Hamish in his rear mirror for just that reason. He knew Hamish was real in his mind and was always over his shoulder. Catching a glimpse of him would not be good.

"I am not certain yet, but time will tell."

"'Ware!" Hamish said.

During the war, Hamish had warned Rutledge of impending danger and now was no different.

Rutledge steadied himself in time to miss a horse and rider on the road. As he passed, Rutledge looked carefully at both the horse and rider. The horse was a beautiful gray with a black mane and the rider was wearing a riding habit.

"Nary a foxhunting habit," Hamish said.

Rutledge slowed and then stopped just ahead of the rider, putting the hand brake on. Opening his door with the motor idling, he got down from the motorcar and walked to the road.

The rider, a man dressed in a smart riding habit, came to a stop in front of Rutledge with a cheerful "Good day."

"It is indeed. I hope I didn't startle your horse."

The rider leaned forward stroking the neck of his horse. "No, Jasper is used to commotion. Charles Johnson. And you are?"

"Ian Rutledge; do you ride this road often?"

"From time to time. I live just south of Maidstone in Coxheath. Jasper and I enjoy a good ride in the countryside."

"You are ten miles from home; that is a good distance," Rutledge replied.

"We'll have about thirty miles in before we get back to the stables. Right, Jasper? It is good to keep him used to being ridden," Johnson said.

"Do you take him foxhunting?"

"No, I have a special horse for hunting."

"Ever come this way with that horse?" Rutledge inquired.

"See here, you are asking a lot of questions for a man I just met," Johnson said with some frustration.

Rutledge reached in his coat and brought out his identification. "Chief Inspector Rutledge from the Yard. A man may have been harmed by a horse around here and so I ask again, do you ever ride your hunting horse in this area?"

"No, I do not, and that is Sir Charles Johnson," Johnson said with his color rising in his face.

"I am not accusing you of anything, Sir Charles. Have you seen anyone else riding a horse in this area?"

"Not often. A few farmers and they usually have the horse pulling a cart or some farm things."

"When you go foxhunting, does anyone from this area join in the meet?"

"No, I can't say I know any fellow hunters from here. I can ask my cousin Elizabeth who lives here in the village and raises foxhounds."

"Is her last name Johnson?" Again, Rutledge sensed Johnson's irritation rising.

"No! She is married to Henry White. They lost their only son during the war. He's never been the same since; he is so bitter. They live up by the Saint John the Baptist Church. Will that be all, Chief Inspector?"

"Thank you for taking the time to speak with me and helping me get to know the area. I hope you have a good ride, Sir Charles."

"Good day to you," Johnson replied and waited for Rutledge to move off with his motorcar.

As Jasper and Sir Charles began to fade into the background, Hamish spoke up.

"Yon man nary like having his ride interrupted."

"I am certain he did not!" Rutledge replied.

Rutledge began to enter Hartsham and decided it would be a good time to meet the Rector. At the High, Rutledge turned right and then left on Church Street. Eventually the street, now Church Road, ended at Morley Road. As Rutledge began east on Morley Road, from his view it appeared he was in the country, not the village, which seemed to have faded a few miles back. On his left was the church cemetery and just ahead he could see the tower of a church. As he neared, he could see a Norman-style stone church with the tower at the front, topped with a flagpole flying the Union Jack. Attached to the tower was another tower that was much smaller, with merlons and crenels along its top and a weathervane. Rutledge recognized it as a stair tower.

From outside the wall Rutledge could also see the entire side of the church. It had matching merlons and crenels along the side wall above where the roof attached. The opposite end was to the east, with the bell tower to the west as usual. The church had a shingled red brick roof that was very high and pointed. A chapel was built along the south side.

Rutledge parked as much off the road as he dared next to the stone wall surrounding the church and cemetery, switched off the ignition, set the hand brake, and got down from his motorcar. The low stone wall had an entrance and a path leading up to the chapel door. Rutledge passed under the wood lych-gate and proceeded to the entrance. Once inside the nave, Rutledge saw the arches were wide and almost Romanesque, but for the point at the top of the arches, with octagonal columns and molded capitals and bases. The seating was divided into two long sections with two side aisles and the central aisle leading to the crossing. The ceiling had exposed timbers. The rood screen was simply carved, and parishioners could see the altar and apse through the screen. An older gentleman wearing the vestments of a Vicar stopped checking the book racks on the backs of the pews and looked up at Rutledge.

"Good afternoon, may I be of help?" the man asked Rutledge.

Walking over, Rutledge replied, "Good afternoon to you. I was wondering if we could speak for a moment."

"Certainly." As they got closer Rutledge took the outstretched hand. "I am Reginald Evans, the Vicar of this church, and who might you be?"

"Rutledge. I am from Scotland Yard."

"I see. Have a seat here on the pew and we can talk," the Vicar said as he sat on the pew. "There now, what can I do for you and Scotland Yard?"

"I arrived in Hartsham last night for a case involving Lord Braxton and the area is not well-known to me," Rutledge replied.

"Ah, the Colonel. Yes, I planned to visit him this evening early. The Doctor told me he had been called yesterday to see to the Colonel, but he asked me to wait so his Lordship could rest. Nothing life-threatening he told me, so I waited until today. I understood it involved a horse that kicked him in the head?"

"Indeed. I am certain that Lord and Lady Braxton will appreciate your visit. I assume they are well-known in the Hartsham community," Rutledge replied.

"They are pillars of the community. Very kind people. And attend this church regularly. What else can I tell you?"

"Oh, I almost ran into Sir Charles Johnson on the road back to Hartsham just now. He was riding through the countryside on his horse. I understand his cousin and her husband Mr. and Mrs. White live near this church?"

"Yes, they do, just down the road from the church. They have an orchard and some farmland on their property. View Trees is the name of their estate. If you go east on Morley Road, the estate name is on a low stone wall that surrounds the property. Elizabeth White helps out here at the church and they are regular attendees. Right now, she is getting things together for wassailing, when our parishioners go to the various houses door-to-door, singing carols and sharing bowls of wassail, the traditional hot drink. We are lucky to have them in our flock."

"How long have you been the Vicar of this parish?"

"Let me see, I came to Hartsham in 1900 so that will be about twenty years. I received the call to become the Vicar here when I was at a small village near Oxford. My wife Agnes and I were pleased to come to this fine church. It dates back to the late eleventh or twelfth century, with some additions in the fifteenth century. The church has its issues keeping it up and all. Thankfully, the Stede Family Trust helps maintain the church. In the past many years, the Stede family has left monies to the church. Many members of the illustrious family are buried under the chancel floor, even Sir William Stede is laid to rest here in our church. He went to be with our Lord in 1671. You will find there is a lot of history in this small village church. Our village is even listed in the Doomsday Book," the Vicar said with obvious pride.

"Thank you, Vicar, for your time and information. You seem to enjoy your work here," said Rutledge, rising to his feet.

"I do indeed. Frankly, you could say, I am besotted with this old church. I wish you well on your investigation and safe passage back to London when you have completed everything." The Vicar rose to shake Rutledge's hand.

Rutledge was almost to the door when he turned to say, "Vicar, is there much foxhunting around Hartsham?"

The Vicar looked toward Rutledge with his eyebrows raised. "Not since the Stede family died out or moved on in, let me see, 1901? I think. It is quite popular in the more west part of Kent toward Surrey."

"Thank you again, Vicar. Have a good afternoon," Rutledge said and then turned to go out the south door.

Back at his motorcar Rutledge continued east on Morley Road. He was looking for a place to turn around without getting his tires mired in the snow and mud. After a mile or so he slowed at a low stone wall and entrance to a farm. It fit Rutledge's purpose perfectly. Turning the motorcar into the drive, Rutledge backed out onto the road to return the way he came. Suddenly, he noticed a worn name on the stone entrance. Looking closely, it said View Trees. So this was the place where the White family lived and raised foxhounds. Rutledge turned into the farm road that led back away from the main road. After passing some toolsheds where the carts and implements were kept, Rutledge could hear hounds in their cages announcing his arrival. Finally, he pulled up to the house. It was red brick with a slate roof and at some point it had been the home of someone respectable. The house was not unkempt by any means, there were simply some places around the house in need of repair. Rutledge knew well that good times had not returned to most of England and so many had gone to serve in the cities or the front. There were times when Rutledge was not certain it was worse in the trenches compared to the factories. He had seen the yellowed faces of the women who were called canaries. They got no pension or compensation for their injuries. Rutledge pulled into the front yard and switched the engine off. The hounds were still barking when a woman came out the front door of the house wiping her hands on her apron. She was a stout lady whose arms looked like she was used to hard work.

"Can I be of help, sir?"

Rutledge got down and walked over to the porch. "Yes, ma'am, would you be Elizabeth White?"

"That would be me, who's asking?" she replied.

Rutledge took out his identity cards and held them up to Mrs. White. "Chief Inspector Ian Rutledge of the Yard ma'am. I have a few questions if I may?"

"Aye, I reckon ye do. Come inside, I am getting things ready for wassailing."

"The Vicar was telling me that you were the one who made these things all happen."

Rutledge followed her down a long hall to a sunlit room that was the kitchen.

"I have to keep these spices simmering to get the flavor right for the wassail."

"I have no desire to impede your good work. I met your cousin Sir Charles Johnson this afternoon. He was out working his horse."

"He is a good enough man, little high and mighty, but I have no complaints."

"I was asking him about an incident involving a man who was attacked on a horse."

"You mean Lord Braxton?"

"Yes, have you already heard about what happened?"

"I stopped by the church after getting spices and other things at the store. The Vicar was going to visit the house."

"It appears that a man wearing foxhunting clothes came at his Lordship from the woods with the intent of running Lord Braxton down."

"Something like that. I had other things to worry about and did not pay much attention."

"Sir Charles said that you and your husband raised hounds for foxhunts. And I was wondering if you or your husband had heard or seen anything."

Just then a man in work clothes came into the kitchen from the adjoining mudroom. He had cleaned up and taken his Wellingtons off before stepping into the kitchen.

"We don't speak of the Colonel in this house. Whatever happened to him, he had it coming."

"Henry, that is no way for a Christian to speak."

"I don't care who knows how I feel. He thinks he can come to church and that makes it all right! It will never be right and you know it. He is here and our boy lies dead in some field in France!"

"The Chief Inspector was asking if we had seen or heard anything to help find the person who did it."

"Take me in then, blame me. Our world came to an end that day while he and his generals sat in a chateau moving men like so many toys around on a map. They killed him and can't deny it! Were you in the war?"

"I was infantry on the Western Front."

"So you know how it was. Talk to any of the walking wounded, the ones missing arms or legs. Talk to the men who can never work again who will never be the same. If all you came here about is the Colonel, you can leave this house in peace."

Rutledge looked at Mrs. White, who had her hands on her hips and gave a slight shrug. Rutledge excused himself and went back out the front door. After starting the engine, he got in the motorcar and headed back toward the church. He had no desire to look behind himself at the farmhouse.

Rutledge continued west and then turned onto Church Road and later Church Street. From there he was back at the High in good order and made his way to Percival's Rest.

After parking the motorcar and turning off the ignition, Rutledge got down and reached back in to take his executive case with him. Inside, Rutledge saw Harold in his usual place behind the bar.

"Good evening, Harold, and how are you this evening?" Rutledge inquired.

"I am doing well, sir, and hope you are as well," Harold said.

"I see you have put some garlands and bows up here and around the fireplace."

"That would be Miss Annie, sir. She has been getting in the Christmas spirit."

"Well, it looks cheerful, Harold. I am going to my room to wash up. What time is dinner served?" Rutledge inquired.

"Dinner is from six o'clock until around eight or nine."

"Excellent, I will be down for dinner around seven then," Rutledge replied and turned to climb the stairs to his room.

Rutledge opened his door and did his usual check of the room. While the room had been cleaned, there were no signs of it having been searched. He took off his coat and stoked the fire, adding some coal to the grate. Someone had thoughtfully lit a small amount earlier and the embers caught the fresh coal. As the room began to warm, Rutledge turned up his sleeves and went to the washbasin. He splashed some water on his face and then used the fresh towel to dry himself.

Turning to his briefcase, he took out the files and sat down at the small table. As he began reading the information regarding Lord Braxton, he could tell that Sergeant Gibson back at the Yard had had a hand in pulling together the information. Markum said it was private and for his eyes only, but Gibson was a wonderful source of information and had helped Rutledge many times. Rutledge began reading back over the Colonel's military career. He had been stationed in India and then South Africa during the Second Boer war. Rutledge thought back to his own Army days and the 7th Queen's Own Hussars, as it was now called.

He couldn't remember them serving on the Western Front. He also wondered what the 7th Hussar's uniform looked like, especially the dress uniform. Being a Queen's Own Regiment of Scottish origin, they must have a presence among the guards in London. Perhaps at Whitehall. Rutledge knew that Melinda Crawford would know. While Melinda had been a dear and close friend of his late parents, in recent years she had grown to be even closer to Rutledge.

And as the widow of an Army Officer, Melinda knew many in the upper echelon of the military.

Melinda was one of the most unusual women he'd ever met. As a child, she'd been caught up in the Great Indian Mutiny of 1857, a heroine in the bloody siege that had cost so many lives. She had never looked back, her life taking its course through marriage and widowhood and years of travel before returning home to England. Melinda would know precisely what an officer's QOH dress uniform looked like. Rutledge made a mental note to call her when he went downstairs to dinner.

The Colonel's career changed enormously when his classmate Sir Douglas Haig asked him to join his staff in '08. Haig had started the British Expeditionary Force in response to the increasing state of unsettlement in Europe. The Colonel remained on Haig's staff throughout the war, even after Haig took command.

"He war one o' them bastards who would hav' killed us all given the chance," Hamish said.

Rutledge continued his reading. If he was going to get to the root of the matter, he had to set his personal feelings aside.

Rutledge got up, went to his frock coat, and took out his notebook. Carrying it back to his desk he began to review his notes from his conversation with the Colonel. After lighting the lamp, Rutledge began reading the passages where the Colonel described the horseman's appearance. There was a problem. Rutledge had not found many foxhunting participants in the area except Harry White, and the Colonel's description failed to mention the color of the rider's coat.

Admittedly he only got a glance and was trying to remember through the haze of his head wound. In fact, Rutledge was surprised Braxton knew as much as he did. The Colonel was a man who was accustomed to being in charge. Was his recollection caused by his insistence in always having the full faculty of his mind? If it was someone taking revenge, the who and why was baffling. Any disgruntled veteran or their family might have cause to seek vengeance against the Colonel, but why him? Haig had been the Commander of the British Forces on the Western Front. Rutledge could find no particular wrath among the villagers nor in the Colonel himself. While the Colonel was demanding and abrupt, that was more from his military career than directed at any one person or family.

Rutledge stood up and stretched his arms. His eyes and back were tired from reading over all his papers. He looked at his watch and realized it was just going on seven and it was time for him to go eat some dinner.

Chapter Seven

When Rutledge reached the bottom of the stairs, Harold was busy taking care of customers. There was a sense of holiday cheer among the patrons tonight. Rutledge waited patiently until Harold was able to come to him.

"Good evening, Harold. I was wondering if I might use your telephone for a moment."

"Certainly, sir. 'Tis just back here. Follow me if you would," Harold replied and led the way through a door going toward the rear of the establishment.

Harold stopped at a small table and chair in the hallway. "I apologize for the lack of privacy; we don't have many guests who have cause to use the telephone. It's getting popular so we had one installed. Eventually we will have something better for our guests."

"This is fine. Thank you, Harold. I shouldn't be long."

"Suit yourself, sir." Harold turned and headed back to his customers.

After making his call to Melinda, Rutledge returned to the front, thanked Harold, and went toward the fireplace looking for a table.

"Good evening, sir. Harold said you'd be down fer somewhat to eat," Annie said, seeming to come from nowhere.

"Good evening, Annie, I mentioned to Harold when I came in today that you have the place nicely decorated for the holidays."

"I must admit I love the whole Christmas time. I thought the place could have a bit of holiday cheer!" Annie said. "How about this table over here where it is quiet and near the fire?"

"Thank you, Annie," Rutledge replied, taking a chair at the table Annie had pointed out.

"Will ye be having something to drink while your food is readied?" Annie asked.

"On a cold night like this, a whisky will be perfect," Rutledge replied. "And what . . ." he continued, but Annie was already gone.

A few moments later she returned, whisky in hand. "It's a local brand, but mind you it has flavor and is smooth."

"Excellent, thank you, Annie. What is in the kitchen for tonight?" Rutledge inquired.

"Cook has some leg of mutton with some roasted potatoes and winter vegetables, if that suits you."

"That will be just fine. I need a hearty meal after today," Rutledge replied.

Again, Annie disappeared among the patrons. Rutledge took a sip of his whisky and thought about his conversation with Melinda. Naturally, Melinda was worried that instead of having Christmas with family and friends, he was in Kent on a case. Of course, that meant she hoped Rutledge would come by her home in Kent on his way back to London.

As he had expected, Melinda knew many high-ranking members of the 7th Queen's Own Hussars. They had felt abandoned when the Colonel left his regiment for the Western Front while they were in Mesopotamia fighting the Turks and Germans. That was why the Colonel had no recollection of serving with them on the Western Front, Rutledge thought to himself. Her description of the Officer's dress uniform was approximately what he remembered. He knew the Hussars wore braids on the front of their uniforms on the whole. Melinda described them as a lighter shade of blue than the Life Guards at the Palace and Whitehall. It had silver braids or ropes on the front in a crisscross pattern. The trousers were white, and many wore the riding boots that almost came up to your knee. The cap badge often worn on the epaulet was the typical round badge topped by a queen's crown, with QO in decorative script and the words 7th Queen's Own Hussars around the edge of the badge. Thank goodness for Melinda, Rutledge thought. He took out his notebook and wrote the pertinent part of their conversation down. Returning it to his frock coat inside pocket, Rutledge took a sip of whisky and looked around the room at the patrons and their revelry. They were enjoying one another's company and discussing preparations for Christmas. Then Annie arrived with his plate of food.

"That smells wonderful, Annie. I have definitely got an appetite from the smell."

"What would you like to drink with your dinner?"

"A pot of tea would do nicely," Rutledge replied.

With Annie gone to fetch some tea, Rutledge examined his plate. The mutton was well cooked and served with an ample portion of brown gravy, and the roasted potatoes with winter vegetables added some color to his plate. Rutledge was pleased to see roasted parsnips along with carrots in the vegetables. Placing his serviette in his lap, Rutledge began to eat. In the background he was listening to the snippets of conversation around him.

Wassail and wassailing seemed to be a topic of conversation along with Offering or Boxing Day. The wassail singing was going to take place on the usual Twelfth Night in January. Rutledge was not surprised that wassailing was an important day in Kent. The county was known as the Garden of England for its orchards and hops gardens. Apples from Kent were renowned. It was good to see the usual gossip and arguments replaced with cheerful discussions.

"Was it as good as in London?' Annie asked, again appearing from nowhere.

"The cooks in London do not know how to properly prepare a feast such as this," Rutledge replied honestly.

"Have ye room for a bit o' sweet?" Annie asked as she cleared the table.

"Generally, no, but is there something special?" Rutledge asked with hope.

"Cook made some bread and butter pudding, with a bit of brandy," Annie told him with a smile.

"Very well, you have convinced me. I will have some of that, and a dram of that whisky would be a nice end to the evening."

"Be a moment and I will bring it for ye," Annie replied.

This time Rutledge caught Annie before she disappeared by putting a hand on her forearm. "Thank you, Annie."

"Oh, go on." And away she went.

Rutledge moved his chair at an angle to the table to relax and observe the patrons. In his profession watching people interact taught him a lot about people in general. Observing people relaxing and at ease, rather than in a police station under questioning, was a world apart.

Shortly, Annie appeared with his whisky and the bread pudding, which was still hot. "I hope that is to yer liking, sir," she said, putting the pudding on the table.

"It would appear that wassailing is a tradition here. Everyone seems to be talking about it," Rutledge said.

"Oh, yes, it is a long-lived passion around these parts. Ever been to an orchard and heard them singing to the trees? It is called orchard wassailing."

"I can't say I have had the pleasure. I do remember the wassail singing," Rutledge replied.

"Oh, that be house-visiting wassail, or house wassail."

"Yes, that sounds right. They came to our house and sang. Then they had a pot of wassail they poured into our cups." Rutledge had not thought about that memory in a long time.

"Ye should go to the orchard once; it is on Twelfth Night," Annie encouraged.

"I have an old friend of the family who lives in eastern Kent. I will try to get to one this year," Rutledge replied.

And off Annie went again. She was an interesting woman, always on the go. It appeared she knew most of the patrons she served. Small in stature, but large in personality, energy, and persistence.

Rutledge turned his attention to the bread and butter pudding. It was not hot enough to burn, but it definitely warmed his throat along with the whisky. He could taste the touch of brandy the cook had added to the pudding. With the raisins and cinnamon, not to mention the buttered bread, it was very rich. Finishing his dessert, Rutledge got up from his seat and made his way toward the stairs after thanking Annie and Harold.

Back in his room, Rutledge stoked the fire and added a small piece of coal. Lighting a lamp, he surveyed the room. Nothing had been disturbed since he left. Taking off his frock coat and removing his notepad, Rutledge returned to his chair at the table. He reviewed his notes from his call to Melinda Crawford and considered his next steps.

The very last thing he wanted to do was to confront the Colonel with his concerns about the man on horseback. Considering the Colonel's temperament, it was not a good approach, but Rutledge could not explain the events as the Colonel described them. All of this would have to wait until the morning when he planned to visit the Colonel again.

❄

The next morning Rutledge awoke from another terrible nightmare. Again he was arguing with his commanding officer about the next charge. Rutledge kept saying they were losing too many men every time they went over the top.

"I told ye the verra' same and ye killed me!" Hamish kept saying.

All the time the Regimental Colonel kept saying orders were orders as his face got more flushed.

"Ye ken that war from yer case with this Colonel," Hamish said.

Rutledge looked at his watch and realized he needed to get the day started. Washing and dressing quickly, he grabbed his case and went down the stairs quickly. Arriving in the dining room, he told the young lady he was in a hurry and tea and toast would be fine. While she was getting his order Rutledge noticed newspapers on the bar. Walking over to them, Rutledge saw they were for patrons and took a copy of the *Daily Mail*. It was not his preferred newspaper, but it would do.

Returning to his seat, he saw his tea and toast coming out from the kitchen. After thanking the waitress for her service and pouring some tea, Rutledge sat back and quickly skimmed the paper. He was pleased that there was no mention of his case here in Kent. The local gossip was one thing to handle. Good to be careful.

Then he looked for mentions of Foxhunt Meets. There were several of note, the Old Surrey, Burstow, and West Kent Hunt, the Surrey Union Hunt, and the Chiddingfold, Leconfield, and Cowdray Hunt. Rutledge finished his toast and took a last swallow of tea before rising and putting on his overcoat.

Chapter Eight

The Rolls was a bit hard to start in the cold, but it was running now and Rutledge headed toward Cottams House with his scarf and gloves on to fight the freezing temperatures. Overnight some of the melted snow had turned to ice and he took care with his driving. Today was not a day to find Sir Charles or anyone else out riding on the narrow road. Arriving at the gate, Rutledge turned and made his way up the drive. As he crested the hill overlooking the house he saw Steves, the groundskeeper, walking along the road. Rutledge stopped and exchanged pleasantries before heading down to the house, where he parked, switched the ignition off, and climbed out of his motorcar. After taking off his scarf and gloves and placing them back in his overcoat pockets, Rutledge walked up to the front door. Davies opened the door before he could knock.

"Good morning, sir. May I take your coat?" Davies said in greeting.

"Good morning, Davies. Yes, please. How is the Colonel today?"

Davies blank look was professional and in keeping. "I will let her Ladyship bring you up to date about his condition, sir."

"Thank you, Davies, and is her Ladyship upstairs with the Colonel?" Rutledge asked.

"Yes, sir, Violet can take you up to them if you wish," Davies replied.

"That is not necessary, Davies, I remember the way."

"As you wish, sir," Davies replied.

"Oh, Davies, Steves has the front gate in good order. Are there usually people coming and going from the estate?"

"Yes, sir, we often have people coming to visit along with the usual deliveries, especially when there are social events held at the house."

"Well, I guess Steves must be making certain all was as it should be."

"Indeed, sir," Davies replied.

Rutledge climbed the stairs and turned down the hall to the door of the bedchamber. He paused a moment and lightly knocked on the door.

Lady Braxton opened the door and gave a tight smile. "Good morning, Chief Inspector. I hope the day finds you well." He had seen something there when they first met. Gracious as always, but was she not pleased to have him there?

"I am indeed, thank you. I came to speak with his Lordship if he is up to a chat," Rutledge said.

Her Ladyship opened the door wide and said, "He is healing nicely, and I think he would enjoy a visitor."

Rutledge stepped into the bedchamber and saw the Colonel was awake and propped up on some pillows. His empty breakfast tray was off to one side. "Good day to you, Colonel, I hope I am not bothering you?"

"No, young man. Come in and have a seat. I am eager to know about your investigation."

Rutledge walked toward the bed and sat in the chair he had used the day before.

"Let me take this tray to Violet and leave you two in peace," her Ladyship said. She picked up the tray from the small table by the window and took it out of the room, then closed the door behind her.

"So, what have you learned thus far?" the Colonel said. His spirits seemed improved from the previous day.

"I have inspected the scene where your injury took place in detail. Unfortunately, I was not able to find anything that would help me identify the horse or the rider," Rutledge explained.

"Nothing? You made a detailed examination of the whole area?" the Colonel demanded. His personality was becoming evident again.

"I did an extensive search into the trees around the scene. There were no hoofprints anywhere. That can be understandable, due to the melting snow. And the first concern was your condition. The scene had a variety of footprints, along with tracks where they were evaluating your situation. They wanted to get you indoors so the Doctor could clean your wound," Rutledge informed the Colonel. Steves has shown him the place where the incident happened. He had helped Rutledge with his search. Rutledge made a mental note to go along with the gate repairs.

"Damn it, man. You should have been at the scene the day you arrived," the Colonel snarled.

"Sir, I received a message from the Chief Superintendent in the evening and drove all night to get here. By the time I arrived it was dark and any investigation would have been impossible," Rutledge replied in as factual a manner he could muster.

"I know. You made your excuses yesterday, but it should have been sooner," the Colonel replied.

Rutledge was trying to be as diplomatic as possible, all the while his mind was swirling with memories of the war. His nightmares showed him trying to end the senseless orders to go over the top. Hamish was right; Rutledge had executed him for the same reason.

"I have investigated the nearest places where any foxhunt people live in the area. The nearest one I could find was

Sir Charles Johnson, and he lives in Coxheath," Rutledge explained.

"Do not worry about him. Besides his stupidity, he does not have the eyes of the man I saw. I have known Sir Charles for many years. We used to attend the West Kent Meet together. I would have recognized Sir Charles if it had been him on that horse. I am telling you not to waste your time," the Colonel explained.

"Do you know anyone else that attends these foxhunt meets who lives in the area?'

"I would have told you yesterday, so again, no, I do not," the Colonel snapped again.

"My apologies, Colonel. So far, I am not learning much that can help find the person who was on that horse."

"I should have known better when I called the Chief Constable. Frankly, I do not think you will resolve this until I am dead," the Colonel observed.

"What makes you think this man will try again?" Rutledge asked.

"I know it in my bones, my good man. I will not live to see another Christmas and that day is rapidly approaching." The Colonel seemed to be resigned to his fate. "Now I am having these confounded dreams that wake me in the middle of the night."

"Ye ken that feeling," Hamish said.

"What dreams are those Colonel, if I may ask?" Rutledge inquired.

"It makes no sense. Yesterday I was talking to you about the Christmas celebrations from when we were children. I had a dream about that the night you arrived in Hartsham. Last night it was about everyone enjoying themselves and having a very merry Christmas. The room was decorated with garlands of evergreen with red velvet ribbons. Someone had put mistletoe on the bottoms of the chandeliers. Everyone was enjoying the season and they were having fun. It was not Twelfth Night because there was no wassail. But I am certain it was Christmas. I was on the outside looking in through the window, rather than inside making merry with the people," the Colonel said.

"Did you know the people inside who were making merry?"

"Some of them I recognized from a long time ago, back when we held large Christmas parties here at Cottams House."

"You were alone outside looking into the party?" Rutledge asked.

"No, I felt as if someone was there, explaining everything I was seeing. Confounded nonsense if you asked me." Then the Colonel shouted, "See here, I did not send for you to analyze my dreams. You are here to find the man who tried to kill me, before he succeeds!"

"I understand completely, that is what I have been working on since I arrived."

"The Chief Constable gave me the assurance the Yard was sending me their best man, but thus far you have no results."

"I would like to offer some protection for you and her Ladyship. I know you have refused it. Would you reconsider? After all it will be Christmas very soon and I would be happy to make those arrangements."

"You may have a man at the gate who can make his rounds, but outside the house only. I will not have Lady Braxton, or myself for that matter, disturbed with constables tramping all over this house."

"I will see to it personally and will come by the house as well, just to make certain they obey your wishes," Rutledge replied.

"Fine. That is settled then," the Colonel said in a more agreeable tone.

"I know nothing about dreams, sir. I do understand that with a severe head wound, resting the mind with sleep allows the brain to heal," Rutledge offered.

"I agree with you. I am a cavalry man and know about head wounds. But it is hard to let my brain rest when my sleep is disturbed with these infernal dreams," the Colonel said almost softly, as if he was convincing himself.

"I know that all too well, Colonel."

"Do you?"

"Remember, I was only a captain during the war. I did not have the command responsibilities you faced."

"You have had your rest disturbed from the death all around you. You know what bothers me most?" the Colonel asked.

"The burden you faced working with Sir Haig, during the war?"

"You would think that, being in the trenches. No, it was my old regiment and what they faced in Mesopotamia and Bagdad. I was the second in command and well on my way to taking charge of the regiment, but I was in France when they needed me the most. I followed their progress as best as I could. They were in India when I left, but then in '17 they joined the forces fighting hard against the Turks and Germans. I was not there for my men in battle."

Rutledge thought a moment and then replied, "I am certain Sir Haig needed your support and assistance with more than one regiment."

"I kept telling myself that, but these were my men since my days in Sandhurst. Haig and I graduated together and, though he was older than I was, we were both assigned to the 7th Queen's Own Hussars. It was quite an honor to serve a prestigious regiment. You know they originated in Scotland?"

"I believe they started in response to the Jacobite rebellion," Rutledge replied.

"Yes, several Independent Troops of Scots were formed for a short-term response in 1689, then under Colonel Cope. It was after the second Jacobite rebellion and Flanders that they became the 7th Queen's Own Hussars in 1807. Until then they were Dragoons. I could go on for hours about the history. Douglas, er, Sir Haig, was very pleased to be joining a regiment with such Scottish history, being from a Scottish family."

"You admired your regiment and gave them many years of service," Rutledge replied.

"Oh, we saw our bit of battles, especially when we were in Cape Town during the Second Boer war. We gave a new meaning to brothers in arms."

"I am certain they were a better regiment for that experience."

"You were not regular Army and don't understand the bond you have after years together. We took our losses with respect and mourning."

"An we had nary time to mourn anyone. There were too many!" Hamish's voice chimed in, always with the sarcastic remark. Rutledge was used to Hamish's remarks though and it made it difficult to relate to the Colonel's fear of an apparition and the fear that it might want him dead.

All this talk of war was getting to Rutledge. He could feel the walls of the bedchamber closing in on him again.

He took a deep swallow before he replied. "No, I was a policeman and an Inspector at the Yard when I joined up. One too many Kitchener posters, I suppose," Rutledge replied trying to lighten up the conversation.

"Kitchener was a good man in a difficult situation. It is like today; the ranks have the benefit of hindsight, as do the politicians and newspaper men. When you are in command you take and give orders as best you are able at the time. Were they the right decisions? Perhaps not, but that is the hand you are dealt," the Colonel said.

Rutledge looked at the sun over the lawn and realized they had been talking for quite a while. He did not dare to look at his watch.

"I am sure they will be up with your lunch soon, Colonel."

"I would imagine you are right. We have gone on about nothing that is pertinent to the matter at hand," the Colonel replied.

"Please know that I am working hard on this case and I will arrange for a guard posted on the property. I hope it is an unnecessary precaution and will not cause distress," Rutledge said evenly.

"Not in the house, mind you!" the Colonel said raising his voice.

"I am clear on that and will make certain they understand their responsibilities."

"See that you do!" the Colonel said sharply.

Rutledge rose from his chair just as a gentle knock came at the door. Rutledge strode to the door and opened it. There stood Lady Braxton.

"Lady Braxton, we were just finishing," Rutledge greeted her.

"How is the investigation proceeding?" she replied.

"I am hard at work on this case. Nothing yet, but I hope to have some news soon," Rutledge replied, thinking it would be best to leave the guards for the property to the Colonel.

"I was wondering if the Colonel is feeling hungry and would like some lunch."

"That will be fine, Louisa, we are finished for today," the Colonel said from his bed. "When is the Doctor coming to change this infernal bandage?"

"He sends his apologies, but he will be here after lunch," Lady Braxton replied. "I will send Violet up with a tray for you, straight away." Turning to Rutledge, she continued, "Let me walk with you to the door, Chief Inspector."

"Thank you, Lady Braxton," Rutledge said and then turned to the Colonel. "I will keep you informed with my progress, sir."

Lady Braxton stepped back to allow Rutledge to step into the hall. Closing the door behind him, Rutledge changed his mind.

"Lady Braxton, the Colonel has agreed to allow a constable to be posted to guard the grounds. I have strict instructions they are not to enter the house."

"If the Colonel does not object, it will certainly add some peace of mind."

As they came to the stairs, she continued, "I apologize for my husband's disposition. He is not the type of man who is like this under normal circumstances. I appreciate your patience."

"I have found that I enjoy his company. His irritable manner shows his sense of helplessness is a large burden," Rutledge replied, hoping his response would have a calming effect. Lady Braxton was used to her husband being abroad for the last years and she would have often traveled with him. It was very similar situation to Bess Crawford's mother, who was also a very competent and capable woman. Still, there was an undertone to their conversation that Rutledge found uncomfortable. Along with Steves's behavior, things were not what he would have expected.

"I appreciate you saying that," Lady Braxton said as they descended the stairs. "I have to be honest with you, his irritability has been difficult. We had already taken the Christmas decorations down from the attics to decorate the house. The staff so enjoys decorating the house and I did not have the heart to make them put the decorations back in the attic. I told them to take them up to their rooms and decorate their own spaces with all of these beautiful items. We all hope this situation will resolve itself and then they can decorate the whole house as planned. Cook has been hard at work on the figgy pudding, and we all hope the Colonel doesn't smell it until he is feeling more like himself. Did you meet Steves, the groundskeeper, yesterday?"

"Yes, with the assistance of Davies," Rutledge replied. Another instance of the way she said something. What was it about the way she said Steves? It was not the usual tone she used referring to the other servants in the household. It was not familiar or inappropriate, more conspiratorial.

Davies was ready with Rutledge's coat at the door. Like so many in his station, Davies had a sixth sense about the goings on in the household.

Lady Braxton extended her hand saying, "Thank you for everything, Chief Inspector."

Rutledge took her hand and said, "It is my duty and pleasure. I will keep you and Lord Braxton informed with my progress. You can always reach me at Percival's Rest. I assume you are on the telephone?"

"Yes, we are. Good day to you. Now, I must let Violet know the Colonel is ready for lunch." With that she turned and headed into the interior of the house. Again, there was something in her tone that worried him. Lady Braxton was gracious as always, but there was something in her speech and manner that belied her words. It almost appeared as if she did not like having him there.

"Here is your coat, sir," Davies said, holding out Rutledge's coat for him to put on.

"Thank you, Davies. I hope you have a good afternoon."

"And you as well, sir," Davies said, opening the door for Rutledge.

Rutledge stepped outside into the cold air and reached to take out his gloves and scarf. A cold wind was blowing across the snow-covered lawn. Lady Braxton had left him concerned. Rutledge walked to his motorcar and, in spite of the cold, managed to get the engine running. His motorcar had kept him going since he got back from the war, without him having to ride the claustrophobic trains. Even this cold weather did not keep the engine from purring. Getting up into his driving seat, Rutledge turned to head out the drive and head toward the High. He was hoping Officer James Wilson might be in Hartsham.

Chapter Nine

Driving slowly down the High, the holiday decorations were very cheerful and the street was busy with shoppers, children, and businessmen. Rutledge kept his eye out for the officer's custodian helmet. At last, he recognized James Wilson shooing some children away from a shop window where they were looking at all the treats. Rutledge looked ahead for a place to park, found a spot, and pulled the motorcar over. Quickly he turned off the ignition and got down from his seat. As he began walking toward Officer James Wilson, the man saw him approaching and stopped to allow Rutledge to catch up.

"Good afternoon, Chief Inspector, ye must be looking for me," he said as Rutledge approached.

"Good afternoon, Officer, I am indeed."

"What can I do for you today, sir?"

"I spoke with Lord Braxton today and he has agreed to allow a guard to patrol the grounds," Rutledge replied.

"Well, sir, I am sure that can be accomplished, but you will need to make a formal request at the station."

"That is exactly what I expected. Where is the Borough Police Station located? I will go there straight away," Rutledge inquired, stepping to one side to let a woman pass with her children.

"Ye takes the High here, which will become the main road to Maidstone. Once in Maidstone it will become Knightrider Street and meet with a main road called College Street. Turn north, or right, on College Street and that will take you to Palace Street; turn right and the station will be on your right. Ye got all that?"

Rutledge made some notes in his notebook and returned it to his frock coat inside pocket. "Yes, I believe I do indeed. Thank you, Officer."

"Oh, please call me James. I am no' stuck on titles and formalities," he said with a smile.

"My name is Ian. Thank you, James. I will head that way now."

James touched the brim of his custodian helmet and went back to his walk and keeping the pedestrians moving along.

Rutledge went back to his motorcar, set the ignition, and went around front to start his engine. Once back in the driving seat, he turned and headed west along the High. Soon Hartsham was behind him and the hilly land of the chalk cliffs was replaced with sandy soil. It was little wonder the berries grew so well here. He passed a few lots of farmlands as the soil became more arable. When he drove to Hartsham on his arrival, it had been dark. Now, he could see some oasthouses and knew there were hops grown in the area. They were a common sight in east Kent. On his drives to Melinda Crawford's home and other places in Kent in warmer months you could see the hops vines growing up the strings set out by the farmers on wooden stakes. There were no stakes at this time of the year, and the oasthouses were silent, awaiting the new crop.

Along the drive Rutledge's mind kept returning to his conversation with the Colonel. It was like a case in Essex he had investigated. A murder with no body and no trace of foul play. The difference here was he had a body, and yet, was the killer real? The Colonel was a man of rank and stature. For God's sake he was a Lord and a member of Haig's staff. Who could doubt the word of such a man? What reason did he have to make this up? There too, after such a serious blow to his head, who knew what really happened? There was Henry White, his dislike for the Colonel was obvious. Was he someone who would act on his anger and take action because he blamed the Colonel for the loss of his son? That would need more checking into, because while Rutledge had seen horses at White's orchard along with the hounds, none of them looked like the kind of horse that attacked the Colonel. Elizabeth did not seem to agree with her husband in casting blame; she appeared to Rutledge to be a solid Christian woman who would not be party to any vengeance. Still, neither she nor her husband could be ruled out. Then there was Steves and Lady Braxton; were they working together to cause confusion? On the surface it made no sense, but perhaps they were protecting the Colonel. Rutledge was not sure about that particular situation.

Rutledge started to pay attention to the road he was on as he was entering into Maidstone. The road had twisted and turned through the countryside. He had long since seen the turn for Weavering, Leeds Castle, and Bearsted and now the road took a sharp turn before merging into another main road coming from the northeast and he headed southeast for a short distance, looking for Knightrider Street. Rutledge veered onto that street and began looking for College Street. It was only a few blocks until he found his quarry and began his search for Palace Avenue. It was a little farther than Rutledge expected, but at last he turned right on the avenue and arrived at the Maidstone Police Station. After finding a place to pull in that was away from the traffic, he turned the ignition switch off and got down from the car.

He stood for a minute to observe the police station. He could see it was built in 1908 when Palace Avenue was created. They had replanned the whole town at about the same time the tram system began. It was a stone building constructed of Kentish ragstone including flint with cement mortar and cement around the windows and main entrance. The roof was local tile and the front doors were a dark brown wood that was formed into a pointed arch to match the surrounding cement with two windows above the door. It was a solid-looking building in keeping with the others along the street. Throngs of holiday shoppers were everywhere he turned, gathering their items for Christmas.

Rutledge stepped up and opened the door. Inside the electric-lit foyer, he walked up to the front counter. Taking out his identification he waited for the Sergeant to finish his call.

"How can I be of help to ye, sir?" the Sergeant asked.

Producing his identification, he handed it to the Sergeant. "I need to speak to the officer in charge if you please."

Returning the identification to Rutledge, the Sergeant said. "Just one moment, Chief Inspector, I will go fetch him for ye straight away." The Sergeant spoke to another officer behind him at the desk and then disappeared into the hall behind the counter.

It was only a few minutes before the Sergeant returned and said, "Right this way, sir," and opened the counter so he could pass through.

Rutledge followed him through a door into the hallway and turned right going through a set of double doors with glass set in them. The Sergeant stopped at an office door and knocked. The door read CHIEF CONSTABLE'S OFFICE.

A voice from inside said, "Come."

The Sergeant opened the door and stepped back to let Rutledge enter the office. "Chief Inspector Rutledge, sir."

The man behind the desk was neatly dressed in shirt-sleeves and when he stood Rutledge could see he was formidable. "Good afternoon, Chief Inspector, I am the Chief of the Borough Police, Edgar Robinson." He extended his large hand.

"Chief Inspector Ian Rutledge. Thank you for taking the time to see me."

"We always are willing to assist the Yard. Please call me Ed. Have a seat," he said after shaking Rutledge's hand.

Sitting down in the leather chair by the large wooden desk, Rutledge replied, "Please call me Ian. I was called in from the Yard to investigate the incident at Lord Braxton's home."

"Yes, I believe Officer James Wilson was called to the scene and submitted a thorough report. I understand you met with him and went over the particulars."

"Yes, a fine officer. We met yesterday and he was most helpful."

"So, what brings you here this afternoon?" Robinson asked.

"I met with Lord Braxton today, and I was able to get his permission to have officers patrol the grounds. He was very specific that they not come into the house to patrol. I spoke to Wilson this afternoon, and he sent me here to make a formal request."

"Ian, you did not have to travel here to make that request, even though I appreciate the opportunity to meet you in person." Robinson took a paper from his desk and began writing. "You need at least one officer to patrol the grounds for twenty-four hours a day for the next . . . ?" And Robinson stopped, looking up at Rutledge.

"I hope to have this wrapped up in a few days. It shouldn't take very long," Rutledge replied.

"I will put this down for the next three days. Just contact me on the telephone," Robinson said as he completed writing and signing the paper. "Consider it done, Ian. It will take a couple hours before they are on post."

"Thank you, Ed. You may want to note that I will be checking in with them regularly," Rutledge said.

"They will be reporting to you and Officer Wilson. Wilson will file the reports to this office, and you can direct them as you see the need. I will pass this on the shift commanders for assignment."

Rutledge rose from his seat and stepped closer to Robinson. "Thank you for your time," Rutledge said, shaking his hand.

"I wish all my requests were this simple. If there is anything else I can do for you, don't hesitate to telephone me here."

Rutledge reached the door and turned back to Robinson. "A quick personal question, if I may."

"Certainly, Ian, what can I do?"

"My regiment from the war is holding a reunion soon and I did not pack my dress uniform. Is there anywhere hereabouts where I can rent one?" Rutledge asked.

"Were you an officer, I assume?"

"Yes, a Captain."

Robinson shook his head as he thought it over. "Not anywhere hereabouts. You would need to go to London and if that is where you live, you can just get yours," Robinson said.

"That is what I thought. Thank you anyway. You have a good evening."

"You as well, Ian, and best of luck with your investigation," Robinson said as he sat down behind his desk.

Rutledge went back to the front counter and thanked the Sergeant as he exited the building. It was getting dark and Rutledge quickly started the engine and got into the driving seat. He was eager to get back to Hartsham. By the time he left Maidstone proper it was getting dark. Again the road looked as it did on his drive just two nights before. Fortunately he was not driving from London as he had that night. Rutledge watched the road with care for places where the ice and snow that had melted during the day was now black ice. Hamish was not helping.

"Ye ken ye hate yon man, and no admit it," Hamish said from his usual seat.

Chapter Ten

The headlamps seemed to narrow, and Rutledge felt like he was in a tunnel with the war all around him. He kept shaking his head to clear his vision. It was not going to be a pleasant trip to Hartsham. Eventually, to his relief Rutledge came onto the High and slowed for the pedestrians who were still trying to pick up the last items for their Christmas celebrations. Rutledge would have preferred a nice supper by the fire at Percival's Rest. Instead he headed out to Cottams House. He couldn't figure out why he was so concerned about the Colonel. Hamish had been right; Rutledge had every reason to hate the Colonel and everyone else in HQ. There was something there more than doing his duty as a policeman.

Rutledge continued to make his way through the countryside until he finally reached the gate at Cottams House. He was surprised to see Officer Wilson standing at the gate smoking a pipe. When Wilson recognized Rutledge's motorcar, he knocked his pipe out on the heel of his boot and put his it in his coat pocket.

"Good evening, Wilson. I did not expect to see you here."

"Well, ye spoke to the Chief over an hour ago and they got a hold of me straight away. We try to be an efficient lot," Wilson said with a wry smile.

"I had no idea they would add this onto your duties. I can call and make a change . . ." Rutledge stammered.

"Nay, I am not here for that. I am just keeping an eye on the place until the other officers arrive," Wilson explained.

"That is a relief. You have many other responsibilities it would be a shame to take you from them," Rutledge said. "So, all is quiet then?"

"Nary a peep. I have seen the lights moving inside the house. It would appear they are getting ready for dinner."

"Are you familiar with the grounds here?" Rutledge asked Wilson.

"It has been a while, and the estate is rather large. I have patrolled round the house and the chapel."

"I did not know there was a chapel here. I suppose it is not unusual for a home of this size to have a family chapel or some ancient church on the property. I had no idea there was one at Cottams House."

"Aye, it is very old, but there again there is a lot of that round these parts. Saint John the Baptist was built at the end of the tenth century or so. Cottams dates back to Elizabethan times."

"Do you have time to show me where it is? Or are you waiting for the other officers?" Rutledge asked. He had two reasons to see the chapel. His godfather was an architect and spent a lot of time teaching him architecture, but it also gave Rutledge an opportunity to see the layout of the estate, which he needed if he was to check on the officers in the dark.

"I expect them a bit later. With shift change it will be a while before they arrive," Wilson answered.

"Why don't I take you in the motorcar as far as we can and then we can return shortly."

"Since ye're already in the motorcar with the engine running, I would love to take a ride in this beauty."

"Come around and climb aboard."

Wilson came around the bonnet, the headlamps shining on his uniform, and then he opened the front passenger door. When he was up in the seat, Rutledge let out the clutch and slowly turned into the drive. As they crested the hill, Wilson pointed to a small farm road that turned off to the side of the house.

"I did not see that road until you pointed it out. It was covered in snow the first day I arrived," Rutledge said to Wilson.

Rutledge carefully followed the road around and behind the house. Following the headlamps it seemed very close in around the motorcar.

"The chapel must be quite a distance from the house."

"Aye, it is. You haven't come to the farm buildings yet," Wilson said. "Once we pass the stables, mind the road, there are some deep ruts that may have ice in them."

Finally, they came to a bend in the road and Rutledge could make out the stables and the toolshed. Out of sight from the house it was a whole different world. The fields and orchards lay open past the toolshed as best Rutledge could make out in the dark. He began to wonder if Wilson was taking him on a goose chase.

"How much father do you think?" Rutledge asked Wilson.

"Not much farther, you will be able to make it out soon," Wilson replied.

At last Rutledge came around a curve and the small Saxon chapel came into view. The grass was tall in places but, in all, the chapel was in surprisingly good shape. Saint Augustine came to Kent from Rome to convert the Anglo-Saxons and King Æthelberht in the first century. Rutledge knew this history from Melinda Crawford and spending time in Kent. He had seen the Anglo-Saxon Church in Dover and Saint Laurence's Church. This chapel, as best as he could tell, had no Norman Tower. A simple rectangular building with a few arched windows. The rectangle faced east to west with the entrance on the west wall. Rutledge pulled to a stop and set the hand brake. After turning the ignition off, he got down from the motorcar and went to fetch his Wellingtons and torch from the boot. Wilson came around the rear of the motorcar.

"I didn't expect you would want to go inside," he said to Rutledge.

Rutledge looked up with a grin. "Might as well while we are here. I understand you want to keep an eye out for the officers from Maidstone. I won't take long."

"Suit yourself then," Wilson replied.

Rutledge could see he was anxious. With his Wellingtons on he turned on his torch and headed to the chapel. A stile was built into the stone wall surrounding the chapel. Rutledge assumed that at some time it kept animals out. He knew better than to try the gate, which was rusted and in need of repair. Over the wall at last, he approached the wooden door, which to his surprise was unlocked and opened with little effort. Inside were a few rough-hewn pews, a baptismal font, and a simple altar with a cross carved from stone on a table again of carved stone. The windows were not stained glass and that is all Rutledge could determine with his torch reflecting its light off the windows.

The ceiling had exposed timbers that led to the floor on either side. It was a very simple chapel that in its day held no more than ten or fifteen people. Satisfied, Rutledge turned and looked at the west interior. The broad arches that came to a point reminded him of the construction of Saint John the Baptist Church he had seen the day before. Wasting no time Rutledge emerged from the chapel and closed the door with care. In the yard was a tabletop tombstone set on ornamental legs with a base. Rutledge remembered these from his family church. Originally the families took an active part in caring for their dead: flowers were kept up, tombstones were scrubbed and cleaned. And rather than mourners standing, hands clasped, as they whispered conversations with the dead, picnics and celebrations were held among the stones. Once over the stile, he could see Wilson was thankful they could return to the entrance of Cottams House to greet the incoming officers.

"Did ye see what ye wanted?" Wilson asked, trying to hide his impatience.

"I did indeed. Thank you, Wilson, for obliging me. I noticed the tabletop tombstone that seems well looked after."

"Yes, that is the grave of the first Lord Braxton. It has a special meaning for the family. As the first Lord, he is the patriarch of the family."

"If you will be kind enough to crank the engine when I get the ignition turned on, I would appreciate your help."

Wilson came around the bonnet and leaned over the crank and then looked at Rutledge. After climbing back to his seat and turning the ignition on, Rutledge gave a nod back. Wilson cranked the engine as if he had done it many times. As he returned to the front passenger seat, Rutledge adjusted the idle and then turned the motorcar around.

"We can follow our tracks back now," Wilson said.

Rutledge still took his time to be careful. This was neither the time or place for him to get the motorcar stuck. Eventually, they rounded the stables and toolshed. Rutledge could then head back toward the house and front drive. When they returned to the main gate, there was no sign the officers had arrived. Rutledge turned his car facing the road from Hartsham and left his headlamps lit so the lorry from Maidstone would see where they were. Wilson got down from the motorcar.

"I hope ye don't mind," he asked holding up the pipe in his hand.

"Not at all, Wilson, go right ahead," Rutledge said.

Wilson pulled a leather pouch from his coat pocket and filled his pipe. Rutledge went to the boot and changed out of his Wellingtons and put them and his torch neatly inside. Coming back around the motorcar, he saw Wilson lighting his pipe with a trench lighter.

"I would have thought you were not able to serve in the trenches at the Western Front," Rutledge said, recognizing it immediately.

"Nay, I am too old and they needed me on the force when the young men left for war. This lighter is from my nephew who served there. His parents were long gone and they sent his effects to me and my wife. I carry it as a reminder of him. That is pretty much about all we have from him as a young man," Wilson said somberly, with a sad look on his face as he held it up in the light of the headlamps.

"Ye got more o' me than ye bargained for, didn't ye?" Hamish said to Rutledge.

"We lost so many young men in that war," Rutledge replied.

"Did ye serve during the war?" Wilson asked quietly.

"In an infantry regiment on the Western Front."

"They don't say much, those that were there."

"No point. We did what we had to do. Why make others who were not there suffer? They gave enough on the home front," Rutledge replied. Deep down he knew the shame he bore every day. Why was he spared and men like Hamish were not? Why did the nightmares and all his other issues haunt him? He had not bargained for all that. Buried face down over Hamish's dead body by the shell that took all of his men. By rights he should be there with them laid to rest in France, at the Thiepval Memorial. Rutledge shook his head in an effort to clear his mind. It was just in time too. A lorry like the troop lorries from the war came around the curve and Wilson flagged them down. The lorry slowed and eased out of the roadway near Rutledge and Wilson.

The driver switched off the ignition and the engine went quiet. As he got down from the lorry, two uniformed officers jumped down from the back.

They came up to Wilson and the driver said, "It was a bit longer drive than I expected, James. Sorry it too so long." He shook Wilson's hand.

The other two men came around and spoke to Wilson.

"Lads, this is Chief Inspector Rutledge from the Yard. We are working for him for the next few days. He is staying at Percival's Rest in town and will drop by here from time to time. I will take you two around the grounds, so you know the lay of the land. Remember, we are not to go in the house unless we are asked to come in for an emergency. Have you got it?"

The two officers nodded their understanding.

"Chief Inspector, anything you want to add?" Wilson asked.

"You all know my name, what are yours?" Rutledge asked.

The driver spoke up first. "I am Clifford Walker and this gentleman with the mustache is Tom Clarke and this large fella is Jack Hughes."

Each one touched the brim of their custodian helmets in turn.

"As Wilson said, I will be at Percival's Rest on West Street here in Hartsham. They are on the telephone if it is an emergency and you or his Lordship's family need me in a hurry."

Each man nodded in turn.

"Well, Chief Inspector, I am going to take these men around the grounds," Wilson said.

"Thank you, Wilson, I am going back to Hartsham to freshen up." Then looking at the Officers, he said, "I will be back by later. I appreciate your help with this matter."

As Wilson turned to his men, Rutledge went to his motorcar and, after starting the engine, headed for the village. He knew Hamish would have a lot to say on his short journey back to his room. Rutledge was almost back to the main road to Hartsham when suddenly Hamish said, "'Ware!"

Rutledge slowed his motorcar just in time to see a man walking down the road. He had a tweed overcoat and Wellingtons on, but Rutledge immediately recognized what he had hanging over his crooked arm: a broken open shotgun. Rutledge stopped his motorcar, hoping he was not braking on ice. He drew to a halt just in front of the man.

"Good evening, sir, I am Chief Inspector Rutledge from Scotland Yard. May I ask what you are doing walking down this road?"

The man's expression went quickly from surprise to anger. "I live on this road and I saw all the commotion and came to see what was going on. What is a Chief Inspector from London doing on this road at this time of night?" he demanded.

Rutledge was paying close attention to the shotgun and whether this man was going to use it. "I have business on this road and do not take lightly to an armed man walking on the road at night so near," Rutledge said. His voice was harsh, but he felt he had reason for concern.

"What business could a man from London have here about, especially at this time of night?" the man repeated.

Rutledge realized he was getting no answers from this man. He set the hand brake and left his motorcar idling as he got down. "Sir, I am here on official business, and you are not providing me any satisfactory answers. If you truly are a concerned neighbor, then tell me who you are and your reason for being on this road."

The man pondered Rutledge's question before answering. "My name is Baden Cooper. I live on this road about a quarter mile from East Street. We don't have any traffic at night around here. You can see this shotgun is broken open and the barrels empty. Does that satisfy you?" was his curt reply.

"It will do for now. What do you do Mr. Cooper?" Rutledge asked.

"I have a warehouse on East Street. We take in harvests from the orchards hereabouts and take them to market. See here, I have answered your questions. What about all this bloody traffic?" Cooper replied.

"Do you know who Lord Braxton is?"

"Yes, I know of him. We work with Arthur Steves and his men when they harvest their orchards. What of it?" Cooper asked.

"Are you aware of the incident that happened there a few days ago?" Rutledge asked, looking at Cooper hard.

"I know there was some kind of accident. His Lordship was hurt by a horse or something."

"I am here investigating that incident and that is why there was some traffic tonight," Rutledge responded. He did not want to spread idle gossip and kept the details from Cooper.

"Well then, I can go back to my warm hearth."

"The night is cold, why don't I give you a lift to your home? I am headed that way at any rate and would gladly take you," Rutledge offered.

"Well, that is a fine-looking motorcar you have there, I do not mind at all if you are willing."

"Come on then and climb in," Rutledge said and he too turned toward his motorcar. Once he and Cooper were in their seats, Rutledge let out the hand brake and pulled back onto the road.

"Is this a '14 Ghost tourer?" Cooper asked.

"It is indeed. You know your motorcars."

"She is in grand shape, this one. I travel to London on business going to the Covent Garden market. I have seen all of the Rolls on the road there," Cooper told him.

"She has served me well over these past years," Rutledge replied.

"Right here before the turn, here on the left. This is my home," Cooper said.

Rutledge slowed and looked to his left. There was a very well-kept home that was a bit more upmarket than Rutledge expected.

"You can put me out here and I will take the walk up to the house. Much obliged for the lift, it is definitely cold this time of year. Have a good evening, Chief Inspector," Cooper said when he opened his door.

As he stepped down from the motorcar, Rutledge bade Cooper a good evening. Turning on East Street, he headed toward the High and West Street where Percival's Rest was located. Rutledge was looking forward to a quick dinner and some time by the fire. Finally, he reached the Inn and parked his motorcar as close to the entrance as possible. Eventually he would need to head out to check on the estate and the officers guarding it. As he walked in the door and hung up his coat, the warmth in the bar was a welcome greeting. After speaking to Harold, he headed into the dining room.

Annie greeted him, "There you are. I was expecting you, have a seat at the table near the fire and I will bring ye a pot of tea."

"Thank you, Annie," Rutledge said and headed to the table where he sat the night before. It was not long before Annie returned with a pot of tea with a cup and saucer.

"Ye look like ye half froze to death. This will warm you up."

"Annie, I must have something quick tonight. Sadly, I have to go back out later."

"We have just the thing for ye. The cook made some Appledore Chicken Pie, with some huffkins fresh from the bakers," Annie said with a grin.

"That sounds wonderful and hearty. I will enjoy that and then I can head back out," Rutledge replied.

"Always on the go, ain't ye," Annie said. Then she was off winding her way through the patrons.

Rutledge had to smile as he poured some tea. Annie was her own woman and got the job done in a most amazing fashion. Rutledge looked out over the patrons and realized he was beginning to recognize several of them. Before long Annie was back with his meal.

"This will warm you up and stay with you tonight," Annie said as she laid his plate and a basket of huffkins on the table for him.

Rutledge thanked Annie and set his serviette in his lap. The chicken pie's aroma was wonderful, especially to Rutledge, as hungry as he was. Taking out his notebook, Rutledge updated his notes with the activities of the day. It had been a busy day, beginning at Cottams House with the Colonel and ending back in the same place. Rutledge was concerned with the Colonel's description of the incident. As an officer who was accustomed to being in charge, he was unaccustomed to questions he did not know how to answer. With his severe head wound, how clear was his recollection? And was his concern over leaving his regiment to serve with General Haig affecting his perception of what happened? Was his memory of a rider on horseback a leftover from his service as a cavalry officer in the 7th Queen's Own Hussars? Rutledge had been disturbed by this since the case began. On the other hand, the Colonel could have been accurate with his recollection. Nothing could be discounted, and that made his job difficult.

Finishing a last sip of tea, Rutledge placed his serviette on the table and rose from his chair.

"Ye're in a rush!" Annie said appearing at his side.

"I have a feeling it will be a long night, perhaps one of many."

"Well, we will always have a kettle on for yer," said Annie.

Rutledge left for the stairs but first stopped at the bar. Harold was serving other patrons, so Rutledge waited his turn. After a few moments, Harold came over to Rutledge.

"Evening, sir, what can I do for ye?"

"I have a situation that requires me to be reached by telephone at any point during the night. Is anyone here after the bar closes?" Rutledge asked Harold.

"I live in the back, sir. You know how it is. Someone has to be around anyways."

"Would you hear the telephone during the night?" Rutledge inquired.

"Oh, aye sir, I have a bell in my room. I will know. Some of our guests have problems or come in at all hours. Sometimes the cook or the staff have to get to a telephone to let me know if they are running late or can't come. It seemed to be a lot easier before the telephone, but that is a part of the times, I reckon."

"I hope there is no need to bother you, but it may happen over the next few days," Rutledge replied.

"Not a worry, sir. I will keep an ear out for it," Harold said with a grin.

Rutledge returned to his room and took his frock coat off and washed his face. He knew it would be a long night. He checked his watch and realized he had a little while to review his case.

Taking out his notebook, he sat down at the small table and began writing his notes for the day. When he got to Baden Cooper, he stopped and thought about him. Somehow, he did not see Cooper in foxhunt clothes using his horse to chase down the Colonel. While Cooper was a fit man, he did not appear to be much of a horseman.

"He wasna on a horse with his gun," Hamish said.

"No, he was not indeed. He was very interested in the goings-on and may have rushed out not bothering to saddle his horse."

"I didna see him as much of a rider," Hamish replied.

"Neither did I, but I cannot rule him out."

That was the issue at hand.

What happened? And why was no one suspect standing out?

Chapter Eleven

Rutledge decided to begin at the beginning of his notes and follow it through, from the time of his arrival at Cottams House to tonight. He spoke with the Colonel, who described the incident as a rider in foxhunt dress steering his horse directly at him. The eyes of the rider were dark and filled with hatred. Doctor Lewis Wright had told him it was a clean wound and not ragged. The Colonel, as he preferred to be called in place of his Lordship, did seem to have overcome his wound and was belligerent in his manner. Used to command, he did not like losing control and being told what to do. The Doctor had shown Rutledge the wound was indeed a clean cut, resulting in possible damage to the Colonel's recollection, likely from a concussion at the very least. Prior to going to Cottams House, he met with the Borough Officer James Wilson, who had responded to the incident. He had been very helpful and described the scene as he found it when he arrived. Lady Braxton had been exceedingly gracious, exhibiting a great deal of patience with her husband and appearing to be highly intelligent, but Rutledge still had his concerns about her behavior.

After his visit to the house, he met the groundskeeper, Arthur Steves, who took him to the scene of the incident. Rutledge had spent a lot of time inspecting the area. He had been especially interested in the location where, according to the Colonel, the rider came galloping out of the trees. While the snow melting in the sunlight and the resulting mud made his inspection difficult, he found no hoofprints nor any sign of a disturbance in the tree line where the rider had come rushing out and attacked the Colonel with his horse. Steves had made a good point that even though the branches were leafless they had sap in them, preventing any breakage. Rutledge was still convinced that there must have been some sign of the horse and rider. He did notice a rock at the scene where the Colonel could have struck his head. It did not match the Colonel's description of events. His resulting investigation about foxhunting in the area and those who participated led him nowhere.

On the road back to Hartsham, he had come upon Sir Charles Johnson. While not from the area, he was riding his horse, Jasper. He participated in foxhunt meets and rode another one of his horses for that purpose. His cousin and her husband lived near Saint John the Baptist church. He had met with the Vicar of the parish, and he had no information but knew Henry and Elizabeth White. Rutledge had gone to the family farm View Trees and Elizabeth's husband hated the Colonel for the death of their son. While their hounds were taken to the meets, they did not know the hunters and their farm did not appear to be the upmarket type of place that would be of much help to him.

In all, Rutledge could not find anyone from the area who was involved in the foxhunting sport nor shed any light on locals who were involved. The Colonel and his wife were well-known and from all appearances were respected members of Hartsham. Chief Superintendent Markum would not be pleased if Rutledge discounted the Colonel's story and had no one charged in the affair. And Rutledge did not want to return to London empty-handed and face Markum's wrath. More than anything, he wanted to avoid the humiliation if Markum were to claim Rutledge's war problems made him unfit to conduct a proper investigation.

"Ye canna' do that, can ye?" Hamish said harshly. "Ye got in over yer head this time. I said ye resented Butcher Haig's man."

Rutledge ignored Hamish and stood up from his chair, stretching his tired frame. Putting his coat back on and placing the notebook back in his pocket, Rutledge headed back downstairs. The crowd had thinned some when he arrived back in the bar area. He saw Annie and stopped her.

"Would it be possible to get a couple thermoses of tea? I have a few men who have been out in this cold for quite a while."

"Of course, it will be just a minute," Annie replied.

While he waited for Annie to return with the tea, Rutledge went to the door and took down his overcoat. He wrapped the scarf around his neck and put on his coat and was just pulling on his gloves when Annie returned with two large thermoses.

"Thank you, Annie, this will be much appreciated," Rutledge told her.

"You try to keep yourself warm, is all," Annie replied.

Rutledge took the thermoses out to his car, switched on the ignition on and went around to crank the engine. Once it was running, he climbed into the car. The cold was getting worse and the wind had picked up. These were times when Rutledge admired the new motorcars that had some form of heater. Heading down to the High, Rutledge turned to the left and East Street came up quickly. Rutledge turned right and began looking at the warehouses along East Street. He was almost at the turn on the road to Cottams House before he saw what he was looking to find. It was a warehouse with the name Cooper's Produce written on the side. It was hard to make out in the dark, but it verified Baden Cooper's claims about his work. Rutledge sincerely hoped that Cooper was in his home staying warm and not wandering the road with a shotgun. When Rutledge turned left on the country road he kept an eye out for Cooper, or anyone else for that matter, waiting on the road this late at night. Definitely Sir Charles would not be exercising his horse Jasper. To his relief there was no one out tonight. Finally, he came to the gate for Cottams House. He was pleased not to see anyone at the gate. That meant the officers were making their rounds about the property. Rutledge turned into the gate and drove to the top of the hill where he could see the house and grounds. Just as he stopped, he saw a pair of torches coming around the side of the house. Rutledge sat in his motorcar waiting for the men to come down the drive. After a few moments he could make out Officer Hughes's large frame. They had seen his headlamps and were coming toward him.

Rutledge got down from his seat and reached back in to retrieve the thermoses of tea from Percival's Rest.

"Evening, sir, it is getting downright cold tonight," Officer Clarke said as he beat his coat with his arms.

"I brought each of you a thermos of hot tea to warm you."

"Bless you, sir. That will make this cold a bit better to take," Officer Hughes said.

Rutledge handed each of them a thermos, which they took with appreciation.

As they poured their tea, Rutledge asked, "All quiet then?"

"Yes, sir, not a thing stirring and the lights in the house went dark about half an hour ago," Clarke replied.

"I am sorry to ask you both to take this on, but his Lordship's family appreciates it very much."

"Would you mind if I had a seat on your running board, sir? There ain't any places warm where we can sit," Hughes said.

"Not at all, it's probably warmer closer to the engine."

"It is that. Thank you. I can't speak for Hughes, but I put longies on when I knew what we were doing tonight," Clarke said.

"You ain't the only smart man here. I did the same," Hughes said. "I dressed as warm as I could and still move."

Rutledge smiled, "Good planning for both of you. Is the tea to your liking?"

"It's warm and plenty strong, just what we needed," Clarke replied, wiping his mustache with the back of his hand. He had taken his gloves off and was warming his hands on the top of the thermos.

"Is there anything else I can bring to you?" Rutledge asked.

"Nay, a spot of whisky would be nice, but we are on duty so that wouldn't do now would it," High said darkly with a grin.

"No, I guess not. Perhaps when this is over," Rutledge said.

The men sat and stood there overlooking the dark house. There was a certain beauty to the scene with the snow-covered ground. The silence was deafening, and Rutledge was glad for the quiet. Anyone approaching would make a racket even on foot. It would be difficult to reach the house with these two on patrol, but maybe not impossible. The policeman in Rutledge looked at the shadows and knew that if someone was determined they could reach the house once they were aware of the guards. Having the men patrolling the grounds provided some protection, but nothing would provide perfect security.

After a while Hughes stood up from the running board, putting the cap onto his thermos. "Well, sir, we best be back at it. Thank you ever so much for the tea. It hit the spot ever so well."

They both touched their caps, turned their torches on, and headed back toward the house. Rutledge would have preferred they patrol separately, but if they did find someone, two sets of eyes were better than one. Rutledge was just grateful that they were there to patrol, so he knew not to complain too much. As they got farther down the drive, Rutledge went around and started the engine before climbing into his seat. He took some care turning the car around without getting the wheels stuck, and headed back toward Hartsham. About halfway to Hartsham, it began to snow, with the wind making the flakes swirl in the air.

Chapter Twelve

Rutledge arrived back at Percival's Rest only to find the place was closed up tight and all the lights were out except one on the ground floor, which he took to be Harold's living quarters in the building. His eyes were adjusting to the dark from the headlamps on his motorcar. Minding his step Rutledge went around to the back where deliveries were made. The door was locked tight and Rutledge gave a tentative knock, no reason to awaken the guests. There was no immediate response, but Rutledge gave Harold some time to come to the door. Eventually his patience was rewarded as Harold opened the door.

"I thought it might be you, sir. Annie said you left a while ago and when I was closing up, your motorcar still had not returned," Harold said as he opened the door wide enough for Rutledge to come in out of the cold.

"I am sorry to be an inconvenience, Harold," Rutledge replied. "Thank you for letting me in. I hope you have a good night."

"And to you as well, sir," Harold said, handing his lamp to Rutledge. "This may be handy going up the stairs."

Rutledge took off his gloves and took the lamp from Harold. "A wise precaution, Harold, thank you. Again, good night."

"Good night," Harold said. Then he turned to go back to his quarters.

Rutledge was thankful for the lamp Harold had given him. The narrow dark stairs and the hallway would have been difficult without it. Opening his door, he checked his room. Again, it showed no signs of anyone entering, except the maid who had put some coal on the fire and turned his coverlet down. Rutledge set the lamp beside the other lamp already on the small table, put his gloves and scarf into his overcoat pockets and took it off. After hanging it on the wardrobe door, he stoked the coals and put another piece of coal on the grate. It had been a very long day and Rutledge was tired. Changing for bed and washing up, he eagerly slipped between the covers after blowing out the lamp. It was a relief and yet Rutledge knew the horrors that came with sleep. A few hours after Rutledge fell asleep, the war came back to him. Once again, he was arguing with the Colonel of his regiment.

"There is no point," he kept saying over and over, before stomping out from the dugout into the trenches.

They were filled with water from the rain. It was up to their knees and waists in places. Ever present bodies of the dead came floating by with macabre grins and lipless faces. Even the rats who spent their days eating at these faces came swimming by. For what? he kept asking these dead men. We are getting nowhere; it is all just a bloody mess. He started to turn and go back to the Colonel when Hamish's body came floating by.

"I told ye, but ye no listen to me," Hamish said as he passed.

"Stop! Come back, damn you!" He was calling to Hamish. He kept trying to grab his arm to keep him from floating away.

Try as he might, he kept losing his footing and falling among the dead. He could not face this anymore. It had to stop. He desperately tried to climb the back wall of the trench so he could run. Run away from this madness. But a hand caught his foot and dragged him back into the trench.

"Ye are gonna get yourself shot doing that!" Hamish said as he dragged Rutledge back down into the water.

"You are dead, I just saw your body float past," he shouted at Hamish.

"I'm no' dun wi' ye yet," Hamish said with a knowing smile.

"I don't care if they blow my head off, this is pointless, and I want out! Any way out, dead or alive!" Rutledge yelled at Hamish.

The shells were flying from everywhere and in the distance, he heard machine guns firing. No sane man was standing here!

Suddenly, someone was grabbing at him, and it was not Hamish. Rutledge kept pulling his arm back. He was finished and that was it. But they kept on pulling at his arm. It was Harold trying to wake him.

"Sir, wake up, please," Harold said.

Rutledge sat up and shook his head. "What is it, Harold?"

"Lady Braxton telephoned just now. They need you at Cottams House right away, the Colonel is missing!" Harold explained.

"Lady Braxton? What is the time, man?"

"Just gone past three, sir. I will put a kettle on while you get dressed."

"Thank you, Harold, I will be down straight away," Rutledge said as he got out of bed. Harold quietly shut the door, and Rutledge could hear his footsteps back on the stairs.

The fire had gone down and was just smoldering as he lit the lamp on the table. Rutledge turned and splashed some very cold water on his face, dried it, and then began to put on his clothes. Once he was dressed, he took his overcoat from the wardrobe door and stepped into the hall. With his room door locked, he turned and headed down the stairs as softly as he could in his rush. Harold was waiting at the bottom with another thermos of tea. Rutledge thanked him and headed back out into the snow, which was coming down at a rapid pace.

His motorcar had a dusting of snow covering the car roof and boot. The front had less snow than the rest of the motorcar, but the engine had cooled down and had some snow on it as well. Rutledge's feet were firmly planted, and he used care as he walked over to his motorcar. As he started his engine the snow began to come down steadily. Soon his footprints from the front door of Percival's Rest had disappeared.

"Not unlike yon Colonel," Hamish said.

"Now his footprints will have disappeared if he left the house," Rutledge said to himself. He was not pleased with the current state of affairs. All the more reason to get to Cottams House as soon as he could.

Rutledge cranked his engine and then climbed into his seat in the motorcar. Adjusting the idle, he headed out onto West Street. Increasing his speed after turning left on the High helped keep the snow from building up on his windscreen. He slowed to make the right onto East Street to head out of Hartsham and then increased his speed again toward the country road that led to Cottams House. The snow was getting heavy as he passed Cooper's Warehouse. Visibility was becoming difficult as Rutledge searched for his turn. Finally, he found the turn and headed toward Cottams House. Here he slowed, not just because of the snow, but to keep a look out for the Colonel or anyone else. He really hoped that Baden Cooper was fast asleep and anyone else for that matter.

Finally, he reached the gate at the entrance to Cottams House. Turning into the drive Rutledge came to the top of the hill overlooking the front of the house. Every light both inside and outside the house was lit. Rutledge reached the circular drive, switched off the motor, and hurried to the front door taking off his gloves. Davies was at the door to usher him inside. Lady Braxton was there as well.

"Thank you for coming so quickly, Chief Inspector," Lady Braxton said, as Davies took his overcoat and scarf. "He went missing about two hours ago. Davies and I have searched every room in the house. We have alerted the entire staff. Steves and the Officers from Maidstone are searching the grounds." Lady Braxton seemed genuine in her concern and the tone she had when he visited the house before was gone.

"I am sorry he has not been found yet. The heavy snow is making it difficult to see and has obscured any footprints outside. Have you searched the cellars and attics?" Rutledge asked. He was hoping for the Colonel's sake he was still indoors where he was out of this cold.

"We have. And I called for the Doctor. Wherever the Colonel is, the Doctor will want to see to him as soon as he is found," Lady Braxton explained. "How were the roads getting here from Hartsham?"

"I am sure the Doctor is used to driving in all manner of conditions. I would expect him to arrive shortly. Percival's Rest is very near his home and I did not see him on my way here," Rutledge said.

"You should know that the Colonel's overcoat and boots are missing from his room. They were on him when he was injured," Lady Braxton explained with even more concern in her voice.

"I want to be certain I understand what he was wearing. It sounds like he is still wearing his nightshirt with the boots and overcoat over it? I am assuming he is wearing them now," Rutledge asked.

"I cannot say for certain that is what he is wearing, but the rest of his clothes are still in the bedchamber. Whether he has them on is a question I am unable to answer."

"If he put on his boots and overcoat himself, do you have any thought where he would go from the house?" Rutledge asked as gently as he could. It was obvious that Lady Braxton was distraught. He was trying to glean as much information as possible, so Lady Braxton could sit down in the parlor.

"That is a question I keep asking myself and I still have no idea."

"One last thing before I join the searchers. Was there a special place the Colonel would go spend time?"

"He would walk the grounds, usually with Steves. He might have more insight," Lady Braxton replied.

Turning to Davies, Rutledge said, "Can you please take Lady Braxton to the parlor and see that she rests on the chesterfield?"

"Certainly, sir. Come with me, m'lady," Davies said.

"No, I want to help find the Colonel. I will feel useless sitting in the parlor while everyone is searching," Lady Braxton said empathetically.

Rutledge intervened, "Lady Braxton, your help will be needed when we find the Colonel. Please save your strength for then. I will keep you informed about our progress and perhaps Violet can come check on you from time to time. It won't hinder our search."

"I will do my best, but the parlor door will remain open. It is bad enough waiting to know something. You don't think someone came and made off with Edward?"

"With the officers patrolling the grounds, I doubt anyone came here. But we are not ruling anything out at this point," Rutledge said calmly. "Now, if you will pardon me, I need to go check with the Officers and Steves."

Speaking to Davies, Rutledge said, "You see to Lady Braxton and I can manage my coat."

"As you wish, sir." Davies turned to Lady Braxton, taking her arm to lead her to the parlor.

Lady Braxton stopped at the parlor door and looked at Rutledge with those soft brown eyes. She said, "You will keep me informed, Chief Inspector?"

"On my honor, your Ladyship," Rutledge replied.

Rutledge turned his attention to donning his scarf, gloves, and overcoat before opening the front door to survey the front lawn, which was now covered in deep snow. It did not appear that the pace of the large snowflakes had let up at all. He was looking for torches that would indicate where the men were. He had not seen anyone on his way in and saw no one now. Rutledge went to his motorcar and opened the boot. He put his Wellingtons on and picked up his torch. Turning it on, he looked in the boot for some spare batteries. He found them and put them in the pockets of his overcoat. They were wrapped in grease paper to keep the batteries dry. He also took out his nickel-plated Kinglet one-piece whistle he had from the trenches. At home, he had his first Metropolitan police whistle from his days walking a beat in London. Rutledge closed and latched his boot and began searching for any signs of the men. He headed toward the east of the house to look toward the toolshed and stables to see if anyone was there. As he turned the corner of the house Steves almost ran into him.

"Pardon me, sir. I did not know you had arrived yet," Steves said to Rutledge.

"I just arrived, and I needed to see to Lady Braxton as soon as possible to make certain she was all right and get some idea what had occurred. Where are the Officers from Maidstone?"

"We decided to split up for better coverage. They have their police whistles and will sound them if they find anything or anyone."

"Do you have any type of whistle, for your use?" Rutledge asked.

"Aye, that I do. I have an old military whistle from the Colonel's days with his cavalry unit," Steves said pulling it out of his pocket.

Rutledge shone his torch on it and recognized the Metropolitan whistle issued to Officers and Noncommissioned Officers during the Boer War. They all had a similar barrel shape and were very sturdy.

"Excellent. Did they have any indication that someone came on the grounds to take the Colonel?"

"No, sir. They were always checking for wheel tracks or hoofprints in the snow. Even now, they keep checking for any prints that would indicate either the Colonel or anyone else was moving about on the property. They were looking for that when they arrived and began patrolling the grounds. Even with this heavy snow that started coming down a few hours ago."

"When were you alerted the Colonel was missing?" Rutledge asked.

"Davies went out behind the house and rang the alarm bell. I was asleep in my cottage down by the road when I heard it. I thought there was a fire in the house or stables. I ran as fast as I could and met the Officers near the front door as we all came running," Steves answered.

"When they raised the alarm, do you know what time it was?"

"I can't say for certain. I jumped out of bed and came as quick as I could. About two or two thirty, I reckon."

"When did Davies say they found Colonel missing?" Rutledge asked.

"Davies said he looked in on him about one forty-five or so. I guess they had searched the house before Davies rang the alarm bell. You could ask him for certain," Steves said.

Rutledge judged Steves to be genuinely concerned and had felt the same about his earlier conversation with Lady Braxton. Perhaps he had misread them earlier and they were working to conceal the effects of the head wound on the Colonel's true condition.

Just then Clarke came up behind Steves, "Good evening, sir. I figured you would be along shortly."

"I am not certain if it is morning or night. Anything to report?" Rutledge inquired.

"Nothing yet, sir. This heavy snow falling fills in any marks on the ground pretty quick like."

"Have either of you seen Officer Hughes?" Rutledge asked the men.

"I saw him about half an hour ago. He was doing the outer areas along the road and around the estate. Clarke here was working the area close to the house and outbuildings while I was working the area between the two," Steves said.

"About the same for me. We were coming to the front of the house every thirty minutes to compare notes," Clarke added.

While they were talking, Rutledge looked up and saw a torch moving down the hill on the drive.

Clarke also looked up and said, "There is Hughes, sir. Like we said, we meet here every half hour." Suddenly, Hughes stopped and his torch swung to face the road.

Rutledge thought Hughes had seen something. In fact he had. A pair of headlamps came up to Hughes and his torchlight went out. It appeared Hughes had climbed on board, and the headlamps came on toward the house. Soon Rutledge could make out the motorcar of Doctor

Lewis Wright. His Austin 7hp did not move as fast as Rutledge's Rolls. It came into the circular part of the drive and stopped between Rutledge's motorcar and the front door. Rutledge walked over toward them and the other men followed.

Hughes got out first, his large frame unfolding from the cramped space. "Good evening, sir. The Doctor gave me a lift to the door. I saw your motorcar come in earlier, but I was finishing my patrol along the edges of the property."

"Anything to report?" Rutledge asked Hughes.

"Nary a thing, sir. All is very quiet in the snow. I was listening for any sounds all the while I was looking at the ground," Hughes replied.

While Hughes was giving Rutledge his report, Doctor Wright got out of the motorcar and reached back to retrieve his medical bag.

"Good evening, Chief Inspector. Any sign of the Colonel?"

"Not yet, but we have an organized search in progress," Rutledge replied. "At present I am concerned for Lady Braxton. She is keeping her composure, but I believe she is distraught and quite exhausted with worry."

"I will tend to her straight away," the Doctor replied.

"Davies was taking her into the parlor to rest. She wants to help with the search, but I felt she needed to stop at least for a while."

"I understand and appreciate your efforts. Let me get inside and I will see to her," the Doctor said.

"Please tell her that I have nothing to report, but we are searching with care and diligence. I promised her regular reports," Rutledge told the Doctor.

"Consider it done," the Doctor replied and headed to the door where Davies was waiting for him.

Rutledge turned back to the men. "We need to stay sharp and aware. I will ask the staff to put a kettle on so you can come from time to time and warm yourselves. You can stop in through the back, into the servant's hall, and they will have tea laid out for you. I know you want to search on, despite the weather, but we will not be at our best, cold and dead tired," Rutledge ordered.

The men split up and resumed their various searches. Rutledge went back inside the front door. Davies came out of the parlor and offered to take Rutledge's overcoat.

"No, Davies, I am not staying. I wanted to ask if the cook could put a kettle on for the men outside. Their ability to do a good search is hampered by this cold and snow. I have instructed them to come in through the kitchen's entrance and have some tea and get warm. They will come in from time to time, but won't stay long. Is it possible for them to take their tea in the servant's hall?"

"It will be a pleasure to provide warmth and tea for these men. Her Ladyship will take comfort to know they have some tea."

"Excellent, Davies. I assume there is not any more news inside the house?"

"Sadly, no. We are working to cover our tracks and make certain. I never thought about how big this house is, after all the years I have been at service here."

"Anything else missing?" Rutledge inquired. "Besides the overcoat and boots?"

"Nothing else that we have noticed, sir," Davis said with a hint of disdain.

"It was very smart of you to ring the bell. It definitely got the men's attention," Rutledge said, trying to smooth any irritation he had caused with his questions.

"That is what it is for, sir," Davies replied

"All right then, I will be outside and come by regularly to keep you and her Ladyship informed," Rutledge said. Then he turned and went back into the cold and snow.

Chapter Thirteen

Stress affects people differently, Rutledge reminded himself. Rutledge turned on his torch and walked around the house toward the stables and the toolshed. He knew the Officers and Steves had searched diligently, but he also knew from personal experience that a second look with a fresh pair of eyes could find things. Looking at the snow-covered ground he saw no signs of any marks or footprints. Slowly he opened the door to the stables. Inside there were half a dozen stalls. The smell of horses and leather brought back memories of his childhood when his parents would take him to visit friends of theirs. He would go out to the stables and spend time with the stable hand. He was always nice to the young boy and let him give the horses lumps of sugar.

Rutledge stopped his wandering thoughts and concentrated on the task at hand. The Colonel was a Cavalry man at heart. Rutledge figured he would make certain the horses were well tended to. There were four horses in the stalls. Rutledge's care when entering the stalls was worth it. The horses were alert to his presence, but not bothered. Rutledge made his way to the two empty stalls. There was no straw in these stalls. The water buckets were empty and dry, and the stalls had been cleaned quite a long time ago.

He turned his attention to the four horses. Two of them made a pair of Shire horses, beautifully groomed and solid black, used to plow the fields and pull the various farm implements. The third was a beautiful Morgan; it had a chestnut coat with a reddish blond mane and tail. Rutledge put out his hand facing up and the horse nuzzled it with its soft nose. Rutledge knew he was searching for a lump of sugar. Patting the horse on its neck, Rutledge looked around in the stall and found nowhere a man could hide. It would have been a risky place. Even though this Morgan was a gelding, it could step on a man by mistake very easily. The final stall held a crossbreed. It was pure black and a cross between a thoroughbred and an Irish Draught. This was a well-muscled horse and a popular breed for foxhunting. It too was well-groomed and appeared to be regularly exercised. The Colonel had a stable hand who understood his horses and how to care for them. Rutledge again held his hand out, but typical of a thoroughbred this horse was skittish and knew Rutledge was a stranger. Keeping his distance, he checked this stable as well. No one would dare hide in a stall with this type of horse.

Rutledge turned his attention back to the Shires. Their stalls would be the best place to hide. Slowly, Rutledge returned to the Shires' two stalls. Easygoing and friendly, they nuzzled his open hand and let him pat their necks. Each horse in turn moved to one side letting him stroke their forelegs and shoulders while Rutledge inspected each stall. Satisfied that the horses were alone in their stalls, Rutledge turned his attention to the rest of the stable. He found the tack room and opened the door. There were a variety of leather saddles for riding. Some were more elegant than others. Each sat on a rack, the leather gleaming with high polish. They showed signs of use but the care that was put into them kept the leather supple. With the various reins and harnesses, there was no place to hide in this place.

Rutledge was looking for horseshoes. In one corner a hammer hung with a hoof knife that told him he was in the right place. Specifically, he was looking for ones to fit the hunting horse. Below where the hammer and knife hung was a set of large drawers. Opening one he found shoes for the Shires. The next drawer down held shoes for the Morgan. They were good shoes that could take some abuse, but they were not racing shoes or for a horse that jumped. The last drawer held the reward for his patience and thoroughness. Here were the lightweight shoes that were used for hunting. Unlike the shoes for a racehorse, they were made with steel and there was an assortment of studs to add to the shoes for better traction. Rutledge inspected these shoes and stud designs with care. He took out his notebook and made some notes along with some sketches. Putting his notebook back in his inner pocket, Rutledge closed the drawers and carefully closed the tack room door and made certain the latch held the door shut. There had been no hoofprints around where the Colonel was attacked, but these would be useful if the opportunity arose.

Next Rutledge turned his attention to the loft where the straw and feed for the horses was stored; a person could hide there and stay warm amid the bales. As a boy he loved hiding in the loft, lying on a bed of straw. He would put a horse blanket on the straw and watch the stable hand working to clean below. He had to take the horses out of their stables and that was no place for a small boy to get underfoot. Rutledge looked around the Colonel's stables. There was a ladder against the wall at the far end of the stable. Rutledge took the ladder and leaned it against the loft edge. He kicked his Wellingtons against the ladder to remove any snow or straw.

Quietly and carefully Rutledge climbed up the ladder to where his head was just above the loft floor. Rutledge slowly looked at the straw and hay; nothing. Climbing up the rest of the way where he could step off the ladder onto the loft, Rutledge surveyed the loft and its contents. Just like the stable below, everything was in order, neatly placed and separated by what it was. The straw and hay were tidily stacked in bales. Rutledge examined each stack carefully. He was looking for a hollow left or purposely created to hide a person. All of these were closely stacked and no one had created a false front to hide behind. Rutledge spent several minutes checking each item, where and how it was stored, checking the eaves where the roof met the walls and where a bale of hay or a bag of food would fit. Everything went to the edge and stopped before it touched the roof. As a result, there was a small walkway between where the items were stored and where the roof met the walls. It was the best practice for storage, so the goods could be regularly checked for damage from any roof leak or water coming in the eaves. Finally, Rutledge climbed back down the ladder and returned it to the place where he found it. He was taking one last look around the stables when he heard the alarm bell ringing at the house.

Quickly, Rutledge stepped through the stable door, latching it behind him. He hurried toward the house. From where he had been, the best way into the house was through the kitchen entrance. Making his way as fast as the mounting snow allowed, he rushed to the house. Entering through the kitchen, Rutledge asked the cook the fastest way to the front hall.

"Right this way, sir," she said, leading Rutledge up a flight of stairs to the main floor. She pointed toward the center of the house. "Ye go down this hall here and you will see the front hall on yer left," she said.

Rutledge thanked her. He hurried down the hall and through the door leading to the front hall.

As Rutledge entered the front hall, Hughes and Steves came in the front door.

"What is the alarm?" Steves asked Rutledge.

"I just got in from the stables."

Rutledge turned to the parlor. Davies was not there, nor was the Doctor. Lady Braxton was standing beside the chesterfield, wringing her hands.

"Do you know why the alarm bell was rung, Lady Braxton?" Rutledge asked.

"They found him. He is alive and the Officer took Davies and the Doctor to bring him to the house," she replied.

"Where is he?" Rutledge asked. He could see the events of the evening were taking a toll on Lady Braxton, who looked drawn, pale, and very tired.

"He was down at the chapel," she replied.

"Very good, I will take Hughes down in my motorcar, so I can bring him back to the house. Can you do something for me?" Rutledge asked.

"Anything to help. What can I do?" Lady Braxton replied. "Just name it."

"Have Violet gather some bed pans for his sheets and lay a good fire in the fireplace," Rutledge said. "Have the cook put on some water for some water bottles. And the Doctor may need some boiling water for his work."

Having a purpose Lady Braxton suddenly came back to life and left the parlor.

Rutledge turned to Hughes and said, "Let's get to my motorcar and get to the chapel; I know the way."

"Remember the snow may be treacherous," Hughes replied as he followed Rutledge out the door.

"If you would be kind enough to crank the engine, we will get underway," Rutledge said.

Hughes went to the crank at the front of the motorcar and waited for Rutledge to climb into his seat and turn on the ignition. Hughes gave the crank a turn and the engine sprang to life. Hughes went to the front passenger door and climbed into his seat. Without a word, Rutledge eased the motorcar forward and circled the fountain to head up the drive toward the farm road. As soon as he made the turn, the slope of the road caused him to let off the accelerator. Mindful not to brake, Rutledge headed down the farm road past the stables and the toolshed.

The road made a turn toward the chapel and soon he could see the Doctor with Davies and Clarke bent over in the churchyard. Rutledge left the engine idling and got down from his seat and went to the gate.

"Hughes, do whatever you must, but get this gate opened," Rutledge said. He turned and walked to the stile and carefully climbed the steps. The others had already cleared them with their footsteps, but there was still some ice on the stones. As soon as he reached the ground inside the wall, he hurried over to the Doctor.

"How is he?" he asked the Doctor.

"Frankly, I am amazed he is alive."

"Hughes is opening the gate so we can get him into my motorcar. As soon as you feel it is safe to move the Colonel, of course."

"I think he is ready to be moved, but we must be careful with his head," the Doctor said.

Hughes joined them. "I have the gate open and Steves is coming down the road. It will be a miracle if they ever get those gates closed again, but we can carry his Lordship to your motorcar.

"Right, not counting Davies and the Doctor we have the four of us to carry him." Rutledge looked around and did not see what he was looking for. Steves joined them. "Steves, I am looking for a board we can lay the Colonel on. We can keep him steady if we move him that way."

Steves thought for a moment, and said, "Wait right here, I think I know where we have just the thing." Steves turned and headed quickly in the direction of the toolshed.

Rutledge looked at the Colonel carefully with the light of the Doctor's torch shining on his face. His color was gray, and it was obvious he had been in the cold for a long time. He could see the overcoat and boots on over his nightshirt. He was slouched by the tabletop tombstone where the first Lord Braxton had been laid to rest. His arms were holding onto one of the legs of the tabletop as if he was holding something with a great deal of meaning: it made a certain sense to Rutledge. Away from the house the Colonel was clutching onto the past perhaps in fear of his own demise. It was as if he was keeping the evil he thought was after him away from the household and he clung to the tombstone for solace, as a place of safety as if he had come to accept his fate.

Turning to Clarke, Rutledge asked, "Was he just lying on the ground when you found him?"

"No, sir. He was on his knees in front of this gravestone holding onto one of the legs," Clarke replied, pointing to the old headstone. Rutledge shone his torch on the headstone and made a mental note of what he could make out. The stone was worn and at one time, in warmer weather, moss had covered part of the words. All that was left of the moss was a smear making the words unintelligible. Wilson had explained it to Rutledge earlier.

Steves rushed up carrying a board. It was the perfect size. "This is the best I could find in the dark."

The Doctor looked and said, "It will do for our purposes. Steves, hold the board while the rest of us roll the Colonel over. I will mind his head. You slide the board in as close as you can without pinching him. Then we will roll him back onto the board. All right, let me hold his head while the rest of you gently roll him onto his side."

The three of them held the Colonel on his side while Davies made certain the overcoat was brushed free of snow.

Steves got the board up to the Colonel, making certain it was wedged properly. Then they gently rolled the Colonel onto the board.

"All right, wait a minute while I check his vitals," The Doctor said, putting his stethoscope in his ears and placing the other end on the Colonel's chest. He moved the stethoscope from place to place around the chest.

"His pulse is thready. We need to get him inside as soon as we can."

Rutledge, with Clarke and Hughes, got on three of the corners of the wood and Steves took the fourth. "On the count of three. Easy and keep him level," Rutledge said.

Slowly they lifted the Colonel and placed the board on their shoulders. With the Doctor taking charge, Davies cleared the way toward Rutledge's idling motorcar. Davies opened the rear passenger door. Inwardly, Rutledge groaned, knowing Hamish would not have much room. They rested one end of the board on the side of the motorcar while Rutledge and Steves went around to the other side of the motorcar and climbed into the rear and stepped over to grasp their corners. It was not easy work. Had it not been snowing, Rutledge would have let the top down, but there was no time. Half stooped, they held their end while Clarke and Hughes maneuvered their end onto the wide rear seat. Rutledge and Steves pushed their end so that the board fit neatly on the opposite end of the seat. They climbed down onto the running board and then the ground.

"Doctor, it may be difficult, but for this short distance would you ride in the back?" Rutledge asked.

"Not to worry, that is where I need to be."

"Davies, why don't you sit in the front beside me? The rest of you can ride on the running board. I will drive with care not to disturb the Colonel or knock any of you off. Steves, mind the toolbox on the running board and the gearshift and hand brake. Clarke and Hughes get on the other side, and everyone find something to hold onto."

Chapter Fourteen

With everyone in place, Rutledge eased the motorcar forward. He was glad for the large engine in his Rolls Royce. In spite of the weight, the engine handled the strain, and the wheels easily found their grip. If it became necessary, the men on the running board could dismount and lighten the load. With this group, Rutledge was not worried about getting stuck so he increased the speed to begin the incline toward the front of the house. The headlamps showed him the way as he passed the house and made it to the drive. He eased the wheel to take the left turn onto the drive and then downshifted as the drive descended toward the house. Finally, he pulled up to the front door in such a way the rear doors of the motorcar were directly in front of the entrance to the house. The men stepped down from the running boards and Davies got down from his seat and went to open the door.

The Doctor had his stethoscope out and was checking the Colonel's breathing and heart. Looking at Rutledge, he said, "He is none the worse for the trip thus far."

Turning to the rest of the men, Rutledge said, "All right just as we did before, let's get the Colonel out of the car. Remember we have steps at the front door, and then the stairs to navigate, and we must keep him level, all the way to his bed."

Rutledge realized the Colonel had not spoken a word. His eyes were still closed. The less he was aware of the process the better, Rutledge thought.

Now they began the process of removing the Colonel from the motorcar. Slowly they worked their way up the steps and into the house. This was the hard part. Keeping the board straight meant that some had to raise it shoulder high while those in front had to stoop down in order to keep the patient level. Slowly, they began the ascent, the

Doctor holding the Colonel's head and quietly instructing the men as they climbed the stairs. At last, the four of them made it then turned and headed down the hall to the bedchamber. Lady Braxton held the door wide. Violet was inside and had the bedding laid back to the end of the bed. She removed the warming bed pans and set them to one side.

They took the Colonel and the board over to the bed and turned so the head and feet were in the correct position. Slowly, they laid the board half on and half off the bed. Rutledge and Steves rolled the Colonel onto his side with the Doctor holding his head. Hughes and Clarke took away the board and with the assistance of the Doctor took the Colonel's left arm out of the overcoat. Rutledge and Steves slowly rolled the Colonel onto his back. With the Doctor holding the head, they removed his right arm out of the overcoat and eased it away from the bed. Clarke and Hughes had already removed his boots. Voilet came forward with the water bottles each wrapped in towels and the Doctor arraigned them around the Colonel's body. Rutledge and Steves gently laid the coverlet over the Colonel.

"All right men, that is our job well done. Let's go down to the servant's hall and have some tea and take off our coats," Rutledge told the men. As they filed out the door from the bedchamber, Lady Braxton thanked them individually. Her thanks were heartfelt.

Stopping at the door, Rutledge turned to Lady Braxton. "I need to place a telephone call to Maidstone. I know these men are ready for shift change, but the lorry from Maidstone Borough Police may have trouble getting through with fresh Officers."

"Please make whatever calls you need to make. Violet and I will stay here with the Doctor. The Colonel is in good hands with us. Please keep the men inside while they wait. It has been a long night for them," Lady Braxton replied.

"Thank you, your Ladyship. They will appreciate that. It will be light soon," Rutledge said.

"Yes, it will, and a Merry Christmas to you all. Perhaps the servants can decorate for Christmas if the Colonel regains his senses."

Rutledge stood stunned, with everything going on over the last few days, he had lost track. "And a Merry

Christmas to you and the Colonel," he replied and turned to head down to the servant's hall. As Rutledge came in, he saw that the cook had laid out not only tea, but a platter of scones.

"Am I the only one who did not realize that today is Christmas Day?" he asked the men.

Their looks of surprise were what Rutledge expected.

Clarke spoke up, "I knew it was today, but in all the night's confusion I forgot it."

" 'Twas the night before Christmas, when all through the house. Every creature was stirring, even a mouse," Steves said sarcastically.

" 'A Visit from Saint Nicholas.' My father used to read it to us as children, even though it was written by an American," Hughes said.

Rutledge was surprised they knew the poem, much less quoted it, with some word changes to fit the circumstances. It proved what Rutledge believed: not all smart people wore suits or a don's academic robe.

"Lady Braxton has graciously asked that you all remain in here where it is warm while we wait for the lorry from Maidstone. She also has permitted me to use the telephone to contact the Borough Police Station so I can learn whether the lorry is able to get through the snow."

The men all nodded and expressed their appreciation. They were bone-tired and cold. Rutledge stepped out of the servant's hall and went down to the kitchen. After thanking the Cook for looking after the men, he went out the rear entrance and stood surveying the landscape. Suddenly, the fatigue and relief all caught up to him. He let out a long yawn and looked out over the snow-covered landscape. The clouds were gone and the sky was turning a beautiful blue as the rays of the sun reached across the land. Every crystal of snow sparkled as the rays of dawn lit them. It was a beautiful way for nature to begin a new day and wash away the horrors of the night.

"A beauty it may be, but we know the horrors that darken our hearts," Hamish muttered.

"You are right, but we all can hope," Rutledge replied.

Rutledge went back indoors and took the stairs to the front hall. He was hoping the ever present Davies might be near and could direct him to the telephone. No one was there. Looking around, Rutledge spied a small table in the front hall by the stairs. On it sat a candlestick telephone. Rutledge went over and picked up the phone. Taking off the earpiece, he tapped the lever that it had held down a few times. Placing the earpiece up by his ear, he listened. It took a short wait, but eventually an operator connected to his line. Rutledge sighed from the surprise that the line was not down somewhere, after the snow during the night.

"Er, yes, Operator, the Borough Police Station in Maidstone, please."

"Please hold the line while I attempt to connect you," came the voice on the other end.

Rutledge waited patiently as he looked around the front hall. The walls both in the front hall and up the stairs held paintings of Lords from years past. The large one in the hall was of a man in Tudor attire, staring down from the wall. Rutledge assumed he was the builder of this house; he matched the Elizabethan architecture. Suddenly, he heard the operator on the line.

"Connecting you now, sir."

"Borough Police, Sergeant Jackson."

"Good morning, Sergeant, Chief Inspector Rutledge from the Yard. I am calling to check on the lorry coming to the

Cottams House to relieve the Officers who are guarding Lord Braxton."

"Yes, sir, the lorry left the station about half an hour ago, bringing fresh Officers to take their place."

"Excellent, it was an eventful night and I am certain Officer Wilson will provide the details in his report. All is taken care of, and the men are fine. Officers Hughes and Clarke did an outstanding job under the circumstances. I will mention them in my report to the Chief Superintendent at the Yard."

"They are a tribute to our staff, sir. I will pass this along to Chief Robinson personally."

"Thank you, Sergeant, and, er, Merry Christmas," Rutledge said.

"The same to you, sir. We have a job that never sleeps." And the Sergeant disconnected the line. Rutledge replaced the earpiece on the lever and set the telephone back on the small table. He went back downstairs to the servant's hall where he told Clarke and Hughes what the Sergeant had informed him about the lorry, so they could have a final sip of tea before gathering their things.

"If you meet me in the front hall, I will give you both a lift to the gate," Rutledge told the Officers.

Rutledge returned to the front hall and went up the stairs toward his Lordship's bedchamber. Arriving at the door he knocked lightly. Her Ladyship opened the door with a finger to her lips. Rutledge took a step back and she joined him in the hall, closing the door quietly.

"The Colonel is resting comfortably. He awoke briefly, but the Doctor wants him to rest. He gave the Colonel a glass of water with a drop of laudanum mixed in it and the Colonel went back to sleep," she said in a soft voice.

"I am relieved the Colonel is doing well. We were all very concerned. The Cook outdid herself with warm scones to go with the tea for the men." She nodded and smiled. "I spoke to the Sergeant at the desk in the Maidstone Borough Police Station. The lorry with the relief Officers will be at the gate shortly. I am going to take Officers Clarke and Hughes to the gate to meet the lorry. I imagine Officer Wilson will be with them. Wilson and I will give the relieving Officers instructions about their duties," Rutledge replied in a similar hushed tone.

"I do not like having these Officers spending their Christmas out here and not at home with their families," Lady Braxton said.

"Whether they are here or back in Maidstone, it is our responsibility to protect and serve. We have chosen and taken an oath to that effect," Rutledge explained gently.

"Well, when you finish, I sincerely hope you will go back to Percival's Rest. You need to freshen up and get something to eat. Then, you can sleep," Lady Braxton insisted.

"I want to be here to speak to the Colonel when he is able."

"As I said the Doctor gave him some laudanum. If you return around noon, we can see what the Doctor says. He is insisting that we not get him excited under any circumstances," Lady Braxton told Rutledge.

"Very well, but you know how to reach me if anything changes."

"I assure you that I will," she told Rutledge with a small smile. Then she quietly opened the door and slipped back into the bedchamber to be with her husband.

Rutledge retraced his steps back to the front hall where Clarke and Hughes were waiting for him.

"All right, men, back into the cold," Rutledge said, opening the front door.

They filed out to Rutledge's motorcar. Hughes again offered to turn the crank, and Rutledge got up into his seat and turned on the ignition. After Hughes cranked the engine, he got up into the rear passenger seat behind Clarke, who was already in the front. Rutledge eased the car forward. He headed around the circle and took the drive toward the gate. It was not long after they arrived that they heard the lorry coming down the road. As it came closer Rutledge was pleased to see he was right. Officer Wilson was in the front with the driver. The lorry pulled to a stop in the entrance to the drive.

Wilson got down and came over to Rutledge. "I understand you all had quite a night here, sir."

"Yes, Officer Wilson, we certainly did. I will provide you with the information for your report, after we get the men sorted," Rutledge replied.

The two officers who jumped out the rear of the lorry knew Hughes and Clarke, who looked tired as they greeted their replacements with joy. There were a lot of handshakes and pats on the back as the two replacements came up to Wilson and Rutledge.

"Sir, this is Officers Willie Parker and Gordon Mills. I believe you remember Clifford Walker, our driver from last evening," Wilson said in introduction. "Officers, this is Chief Inspector Rutledge from the Yard, who is heading this investigation," Wilson said.

Shaking their hands, Rutledge said, "It is a pleasure to meet you. I appreciate your help on Christmas Day."

Parker spoke up, "It comes with the job, right, sir?"

"It does indeed. I am sure you have been informed that we are patrolling the grounds here, but not anywhere inside the house. In case of an emergency, they have an alarm bell at the back of the house that is easily heard on the estate. I assume you have your police whistles?" Rutledge asked.

The officers produced their whistles and Rutledge continued. "You know how to use them to communicate, so keep them at hand. The officers agreed and saluted their custodian helmets.

Rutledge turned to Hughes and Clarke.

"I cannot begin to thank you for your efforts last night. According to Lady Braxton, the Colonel is recovering nicely. It will take some time for him to be back to normal, but the early signs are good. Without you two, Davies and Steves, I doubt the Colonel would have survived."

Rutledge reached toward the Officers and shook their hands. As he was doing so, he noticed extra bulges in their uniform coat pockets. It appeared the Cook sent them home with some scones.

Turning to Officer Wilson, Rutledge said, "Lady Braxton said the Colonel is sleeping. The Doctor gave him something. I will return at noon. Can I give you a lift into Hartsham?"

"That would be grand, sir," Wilson replied. "I left my bicycle in town"

"Excellent, I will give you an update for your report on the way," Rutledge said motioning Wilson toward the front passenger seat in his motorcar.

While Wilson climbed into his seat, Rutledge walked over to Officer Walker. "You did a great job coming out from Maidstone this morning. I hope the return journey is a bit easier."

"We saw worse during the war, sir," Walker replied.

Rutledge looked at Walker in a new light. With the heavy clothing it was hard to tell the age of the man. Now, with his cap off, Rutledge could see his face and hair. He was the right age to have served.

"Western Font?" Rutledge asked, and Walker nodded. "We have seen the worst of it then."

"Aye, no point reliving those years, our dreams do that for us," Walker said.

Rutledge shook his head sadly. Placing his hand on Walker's shoulder he said, "Safe journey, we have not survived that to lose it all on a country road."

"Will do, sir," Walker said, and headed toward the driver's seat in the lorry.

At his own motorcar, Rutledge switched the ignition before he went to the front of the bonnet and cranked the engine. As he walked back to his seat, he noted that his car needed a thorough wash. He climbed up into the driver's seat, slipped the motorcar into gear, and pulled out of the entrance to the drive behind the lorry heading up the country road. By the time they reached the High in Hartsham,

A CHRISTMAS WITNESS

Wilson had completed his notes from Rutledge's description of the events at Cottams House.

"Ye can drop me here, sir. My bicycle is by the shops over yonder," Wilson said pointing down the High.

"If you have any questions, I will be at Percival's Rest, washing up and getting a bit of breakfast. About noon I will head back to Cottams House," Rutledge informed Wilson.

"Ye look like ye need some rest, pardon me saying so, sir," Wilson replied.

As Rutledge slowed and came to a stop at the corner of the High and West Street, Wilson got down from his seat and thanked Rutledge for the lift. At Percival's Rest, Rutledge could not decide whether to eat breakfast or go to his room and collapse. He entered the front door and surveyed the room. There were a few guests eating their breakfast who looked up when Rutledge came in. Harold and Annie met him at the entrance to the dining area.

"What happened to ye?" Annie asked.

"A long night in a snowstorm," Rutledge said, hoping they would not press for details.

"Why don't ye go up to your room and put on some dry clothes and wash up. Annie and I will set the table by the fireplace for ye and have a pot of tea at the ready when you come back down for some breakfast. I trust you are not planning on going back out for a while!"

Rutledge simply nodded and headed for the stairs. Back in his room, he glanced in the mirror. His hair was wet and had streaks of mud that were clinging to it. His shirt cuffs and collar were not worth saving or having cleaned. The rest of his clothing was wet and smeared with mud.

"Ye're no' fit for being seen in your state!" Hamish said.

"Your ability to state the obvious is astounding," Rutledge replied.

Chapter Fifteen

When noon came, Rutledge left his room. Breakfast had been a blur, and he had slept hard. He changed his clothes and did his best with the overcoat, gloves, and scarf. He had left them near the coal grate to dry as much as possible. He certainly did not appear as badly off as he had when he first came into his room to change.

Rutledge went down the stairs into the bar area. Annie looked at him from across the room and smiled and nodded her approval. Rutledge went out to his car, putting his gloves on. After he got the motorcar running, he pulled out and headed to Cottams House.

Rutledge was becoming experienced with the road from Hartsham to the Estate. Soon he was taking the drive and making the circle to the front entrance. Parking his motorcar near the door, but leaving room for the Doctor to get to his Austin, Rutledge got down from his motorcar. As usual, Davies greeted him at the front door, offering to take his coat.

"Thank you, Davies, any word about the Colonel?"

"Her Ladyship and the Doctor are in the Colonel's bedchamber, sir. They will be able to give you an update on his condition."

Rutledge knew that would be Davies' response, but it made for conversation. He turned and went up the stairs heading for the Colonel's room. A light knock was again answered by Lady Braxton, who stepped out into the hall.

She motioned to Rutledge to come with her a few steps away from the door.

Turning to him, she said, "I need to prepare you before you go into the bedchamber."

"Is the Colonel all right? I know it has been difficult to help him recover from the cold and his injury," Rutledge said. He was tense and it showed in his voice.

"He has recovered physically and seems to have regained his senses, to a point," Lady Braxton said putting a hand on his arm. "That is not what concerns the Doctor and me."

Relieved, Rutledge asked, "What is the problem?"

"I don't know how best to describe his manner, but he is uncharacteristically cheerful. He wants a party for Christmas with decorations and a meal with all the trimmings. He wants the leftovers given to the staff for Boxing Day and a carriage ride for them too!"

"Is he delirious? Perhaps the head wound was worsened from his exposure."

"No, that is the same, the head wound was almost healed when the Doctor changed his bandage after he awoke. He is making perfect sense and certainly knows where he is in the house."

Rutledge arched his eyebrows, "What does the Doctor say?"

"The Doctor is the one who says he is making perfect sense. It is just . . ."

"Yes?" Rutledge said in a calm voice.

"You know the Colonel. He has an unusual temperament and can be difficult."

"Yes, I understand what you mean by difficult," Rutledge agreed.

"Well, that has changed. Mind you, I am not complaining. But he is exuberant, and I am not accustomed to his new disposition. Oh, and he wants to see you straight away. I just wanted to prepare you before you went in to see him," she said.

Now it was Rutledge's turn to comfort Lady Braxton. "It will be fine. Sometimes people have a change of heart after a traumatic experience. In the space of a few days, he has had a severe head wound and has almost frozen to death. I have seen this before. It will be fine. Are you all right? Perhaps you need get away from this and get some rest too. I will be fine."

"Ye know all about losing yer mind," Hamish commented.

Rutledge ignored Hamish and stood while Lady Braxton went toward the stairs shaking her head. He was not certain what he was walking into when he headed to the Colonel's bedchamber. He took a deep breath and knocked lightly on the door again.

This time Doctor Wright answered the door and, when he saw Rutledge, swung the door wide. The Colonel was sitting upright in the bed with a gleam in his eye Rutledge had never seen before.

"There you are, young man. I have been waiting for you to arrive. Come sit here by the bed in your usual place."

"Good day, Colonel. You are looking so much better than when I saw you last!" Rutledge answered. "How is your patient today, Doctor?"

"He is well recovered, as you can see. His head wound is almost healed! If I did not know better, I would say the Colonel is a different man."

"You fuss over me too much, Doctor. Please give me the room so Rutledge and I can have a chat," the Colonel told Doctor Wright.

"It would be good to stretch my legs," the Doctor said. As he passed by Rutledge on his way to the door the Doctor spoke softly to him, "I will be right outside if you need me. I fear this exuberance may not last."

"Stop mumbling your concerns to this young man and leave us be for a moment, Doctor," the Colonel said with a disarming smile.

Without another word, the Doctor stepped into the hall and quietly shut the door.

"Please have a seat. Rutledge is your last name. May I ask what your first name might be?"

"Ian, sir."

"All right then, my name is Edward. Let us drop formality and talk for a bit. Will you do that for me, Ian?"

"Certainly, sir . . . ah, Edward. What would you like to discuss?"

"Well, Ian, a lot has happened in the last few days, and I think you may be the only one who can understand what I have to tell you."

Rutledge was having trouble calling Field Marshall Sir Douglas Haig's trusted staff officer, a Colonel in the Army and a Lord, to boot, by his first name.

"I will do my very best."

"We are both former Army officers who know what it takes to be counted on by the men under our command. We know well the hardship of leading them into battle where they may not return. Our careers were different, but our responsibility is the same. Would you agree?" the Colonel asked.

"I follow you. Yes, there are differences, but at its core we share that weight on our shoulders," Rutledge said tentatively.

Like the Doctor, he was not sure this cheerful and seemingly nice person would not again become the man he had come to know over the last days.

"Relax, Ian, I really need to talk this through with you."

"I understand, Edward," Rutledge replied, trying to appear relaxed, even with Hamish muttering in the background.

"I have read your file from the Army HQ, and I know you were buried alive by a shell exploding almost on top of you. I share your guilt. Why me and not them? How did I survive when the others did not? Am I making the correct assumption?"

"In fact, you are absolutely right," Rutledge affirmed.

"In a way, I was behind the lines on the Western Front. I helped make the decisions that took the lives of good men. Men like those in your company who did not come home. Correct?" the Colonel asked.

"One could put it that way. But it was a different kind of war than the Boer War, even. You could not have foreseen. We were all learning and paying a heavy price along the way."

"Thank you, Ian, that is a nice thing to say, but I remember the belief on the Front that the Officers back at HQ were unfeeling and senseless."

"It was a difficult time for us all. Thank God it is over."

"Now to the heart of the matter. What happened over the last few days. Isn't that your purpose for being here?"

"Yes, that is why Chief Superintendent Markum sent me."

"Well, in my confusion over the last few days, I have not been quite accurate in my description of what happened. In part due to my injury and in part because you and I have been able to talk about things that did not have to do with the case, as it were. Your patience in listening to me has helped sort things out tremendously. You may not have realized how important our chats were in this process."

Rutledge was deeply confused and wished the Colonel would make his point. However, he had enough experience to know it had to be told in the Colonel's own manner.

"I am not sure I follow you, but I think if you continue it will become clear."

"Exactly. I have been confusing my dreams with true events. I wanted to believe I was assaulted by a rider on horseback, but your questions and your diligence in investigating my story made me realize what happened. Only I refused to admit it, even to myself. Remember all the questions about what the rider was wearing and all the work you did investigating foxhunting?

"Yes, I do remember that first day. And my questions about the rider's jacket, the second day we talked."

"You realized it was not foxhunting clothes at all that I was describing. It was the dress uniform of the Queen's Own Hussars. Am I right so far?"

"I had my suspicions, but I could not be certain."

"Be honest with me, Ian. You could not tell Haig's aid and a Colonel that he was out of his mind."

"That thought had occurred to me," said Rutledge, wryly.

"Do you remember, without looking at your notes, what else we talked about that first day?"

"Well, you discussed your early Christmases when you were a child."

"Precisely. We talked about stockings with oranges and nuts in them. You seemed to like the oranges."

"Yes, we mainly got them at Christmastime."

The Colonel took a deep breath and Rutledge braced himself for the confession he now knew was coming. "I slipped and hit my head on a rock. Granted it sliced my head and caused a concussion. But I could not get that to make sense to me. In my guilt over leaving my regiment, it became something more. And then, that night, I dreamed about Christmas as a child and all the wonder and joy it brought to me."

"Yes, I remember that you said that clearly."

"I thought I was not seeing anything clearly, and now I do."

"I understand, but something tells me there is more?"

"How right you are my boy! What did we discuss the second day when you asked me about how I was sleeping?"

"You said your dreams were troubling you. During the night you dreamed you were watching a party at your house from outside the window."

"Precisely, Ian, you have an extraordinary memory. You asked me if I was alone. Am I correct?"

"Yes, you were not clear who was there beside you. I do not remember your answer."

"I did not want to say, and I did not tell you. It was a jovial man who was with me. Fat and happy as we watched the party. He commented on the fun my younger self was having."

"But what happened last night and how did you wind up in the chapel yard?"

"Ian, that was the worst part. I dreamed I died. Remember I told you the very first day that I would not live to see Christmas?"

"You were very specific about that. You wanted no Christmas plans made because of your death, which would come before Christmas."

"And I almost did die. Louisa and the Doctor told me what you and the men did to save me. Had you not found me, I would have surely met my end in the chapel yard."

"How did you wind up there in the first place, Edward?"

"It must have been a dream or something. Someone came to visit me."

"Who was it that came to you last night?"

"I don't know his name. He wore a long robe with a hood over his head. I never saw his face. He gestured to me with his staff, and I followed him with my overcoat and boots. I had no idea where we were going. He showed me a body in a bed down the hall and there I was, lying in the bed. Dead. Then he took me to the chapel yard and had me kneel before the tombstone of my ancestor, but it had my name on the stone. Do you understand what I am telling you?"

"I believe I do, in a way. Just like Charles Dickens's *A Christmas Carol*?"

"Exactly! But no one will ever believe me."

"The day we first met you told me how you overheard some young officers talking about the older commanders. They gave them a name and you took it personally."

"Yes, they called us the Jacob Marleys. Ebenezer Scrooge's old partner."

"In the story, Jacob Marley returns to Scrooge as a ghost with his lock boxes and chains. They were forged by his mistakes in life. He is there to warn Scrooge of what his future will be if he does not change."

"Yes, I remember that vividly. I was hurt by that comment. That we were angry ghosts."

"But, Edward, the opposite is true. We veterans of the war are here to warn our brothers in arms not to make the mistakes we all made."

"Ian, that makes no sense in regard to what I have been through."

"It does if you consider that while we must remind our future generations not to make our mistakes, we have also made mistakes that we must atone for and accept if we are to live on."

"Aha." The Colonel paused thoughtfully. "That is why I enjoy our conversations, Ian. I hope this is not our last. I am no longer the man hobbled with guilt. You helped me see that making amends part of it. I let my shame and regrets overshadow the man that I must become. Who knows if Dickens was right in his description of Scrooge becoming a changed man. But I am sure that I can do it, with some help."

"I often come to visit my family friend who lives in Kent, east of here. We can visit and catch up on things when I am in the area," Rutledge said. "You have a loving wife, and your staff holds you in high regard. I am certain this experience will stay with you in a positive way for a long time."

"You are not referring to Melinda Crawford, are you?"

"Yes, she was a good friend to my late parents when they were alive, and she has taken me under her wing so to speak."

"She is an amazing woman. You are fortunate to have her to watch over you. I may be a different man now, but the details of our conversations are between the two of us. Correct?"

"Naturally, as a friend and brother in arms," replied Rutledge, although he suspected both Lady Braxton and Steves were aware of the burden the Colonel carried ever since the war.

"Thank you, Ian. I enjoy our frank conversations and look forward to more. Now let Doctor Wright and Louisa, er Lady Braxton back in, if you please. We have some Christmas plans to discuss."

Rutledge smiled and stood up from his chair to go to the door, knowing that the only witness in this case was the Colonel's own guilt, come to life in his mind, which was hopefully at peace, for now.

"Oh, before you go, do not worry about Markum. I will see to it that he and the Chief Constable know this matter is resolved satisfactorily and I am depending on your good discretion not to file any formal charges related to this incident."

"Thank you, Colonel, I look forward to seeing you again soon."

"Good day, Chief Inspector," the Colonel said with a wry smile.

Rutledge settled his bill at Percival's Rest and said his goodbyes to Harold and Annie. On his way out of town he stopped on the High and spoke to Officer Wilson. He wanted Wilson to call the lorry to pick up the Officers at Cottams House and let him know that there was no need for further patrols. Wilson said he would deliver Rutledge's thanks to Chief Robinson for providing such excellent officers. Finally, Rutledge made it back to London. He had been in no condition to appear at Melinda Crawford's house. He never liked to worry her for no reason.

Rutledge took his motorcar to his man who grumbled but did a superb job cleaning it up. It shined as bright as a new penny.

He filed his report with Markum, who was still not certain about how the case was resolved, but would never question the glowing report from his Lordship. The uncertainty gave Markum an opportunity to say in so many words that he would let this incident go, still . . .

❄

Several days had passed since Rutledge's return from Hartsham, when he came home one evening and found a parcel waiting for him.

Inside there was a note on Braxton Family stationery. Rutledge opened the card. It was from Lady Braxton.

Dear Chief Inspector Rutledge,

I cannot begin to thank you for your efforts and kindness working with the Colonel. His progress has been a miracle to see, and his changed disposition has remained. We both hope that you will visit us again soon.

Sincerely,
Lady Louisa Braxton

Rutledge sat and reread the letter. Lord and Lady Braxton were now people he thought of fondly, and he looked forward to visiting Cottams House again.

Looking back at the package, inside he saw a box wrapped in gold paper with a red ribbon. He opened it with care and took out the contents. It was a bottle of Haig Scotch Whisky with a small note attached. It said only, *"Enjoy! Edward."*